Why Should I Trust You?

Sudeep Nagarkar has authored sixteen bestselling novels: *Few Things Left Unsaid*, *That's the Way We Met*, *It Started With a Friend Request*, *Sorry You're Not My Type*, *You're the Password to My Life*, *You're Trending in My Dreams*, *She Swiped Right Into My Heart*, *All Rights Reserved for You*, *Our Story Needs No Filter*, *She Friend Zoned My Love*, *The Secrets We Keep*, *Stand By Me!*, *A Second Chance*, *Can't Quarantine Our Love*, *Happily Never After* and *It Was Always You*. He has been featured on the Forbes longlist of the most influential celebrities for two consecutive years. He was also awarded the 'Celebrity author of 2013' by Amazon and, in 2016, he was awarded the 'Youth Icon of the Year' by Zee Awards and WBR group.

He has given guest lectures at various organisations and institutes, including TEDx and the IITs.

Sudeep Nagarkar

Why Should I Trust You?

First published by Westland Books, a division of Nasadiya Technologies Private Limited, in 2023

No. 269/2B, First Floor, 'Irai Arul', Vimalraj Street, Nethaji Nagar, Alapakkam Main Road, Maduravoyal, Chennai 600095

Westland and the Westland logo are the trademarks of Nasadiya Technologies Private Limited, or its affiliates.

Copyright © Sudeep Nagarkar, 2023

Sudeep Nagarkar asserts the moral right to be identified as the author of this work.

ISBN: 9789357767590

10 9 8 7 6 5 4 3 2 1

This is a work of fiction. Names, characters, organisations, places, events and incidents are either products of the author's imagination or used fictitiously.

All rights reserved

Typeset by Jojy Philip, New Delhi 110 015

Printed at Nutech Print Services-India

No part of this book may be reproduced, or stored in a retrieval system, or transmitted in any form or by any means, electronic, mechanical, photocopying, recording, or otherwise, without express written permission of the publisher.

Contents

1	Who Am I?	1
2	My New Family	6
3	Usha Soni: I'll Protect Nandini	16
4	Nandini: Back to Normal Life?	21
5	Nandini: Who Is He?	31
6	Nandini: Love or Courtesy?	36
7	Nandini: Trust Me, I Didn't Do It	41
8	Sahil: The Smoke of Love	48
9	Nandini: A Night to Forget	54
10	Nandini: I Miss My Parents	62
11	Megha: He Crushed My Heart	68
12	Nandini: I Need You	74
13	Sahil: Nandini Kashyap Is Dead	84
14	Nandini: Will You Accept Me?	89

15	Megha: Trust Me, You Are Strong Too!	99
16	Nandini: I Love You	105
17	Nandini: No One Can Replace You	113
18	Nandini: She'll Never Accept	123
19	Nandini: Felt Like Home	129
20	Nandini: Don't Remember Your Past	137
21	Nandini: I Saw Him Again	142
22	Nandini: Does He Really Love Me?	147
23	Nandini: United in Love!	153
24	Nandini: I Want to Die	161
25	Nandini: Finally, We Met	168
26	Nandini: Unspoken Feelings	174
27	Nandini: I'll Fight my Demons!	179
28	Nandini: Walking into the Past	183
29	Nandini: Broken Pieces, Unsolved Puzzles	196
30	Nandini: Done and Dusted	205
31	Nandini: Losing Hope	210
32	Nandini: The Final Triumph	215
33	Nandini: Last Nail in the Coffin?	220
34	Nandini: Sunshine after the Storm	226

1

Who Am I?

I wake up to the sound of monitors beeping and of instruments being placed on a steel tray at a distance. I can clearly see the scene in my mind's eye. I know that I must get up. But the pull of sleep is too strong and my limbs feel too heavy to move. Finally, I open my eyes to a blurry vision—it takes me a couple of minutes to focus on the surroundings. A blood pressure cuff is wrapped around my right arm and a pulse meter is attached to my middle finger. From my dry mouth and foggy mind, I can make out that I am waking up, not from normal sleep but from an anaesthesia-induced one. I let my gaze wander around the room. I can see white walls and blue curtains. There are a few vases holding fresh flowers near the window on the right. But the scent of those flowers is no match for the strong smell of antiseptic and sanitiser that hits my nose. I shift my gaze towards the ticking sound of the wall clock coming from my left. It shows the time as eleven o'clock and the sunlight outside the window indicates it's morning. The calendar next to the wall clock shows the month and the year.

26 January 2018.

As I stare at the date, I have a million questions in my mind. The most important one: *Where am I and why?*

I have a strong urge to get up but I can't. I feel as if rocks have been placed on me and force is being applied to push me down. My head is heavy and it feels like someone is hammering on it continuously. I try to recollect what could have brought me here but I have no memory of any past events. It feels like my body is paralysed. The moment this thought crosses my mind, a sense of fear engulfs me. I look towards the door to see if I can spot anyone. After waiting for a few minutes, I shout. Hearing my screams, a nurse rushes in. She stares at me in shock, almost as if she can't believe I am awake.

'Call the doctor immediately,' she says to the ward boy. She turns back to look at me, her gaze unblinking, as if something unbelievable is unfolding in front of her eyes and she doesn't want to miss even a bit of it. And that's when I realise that something is not quite right with me. But what? Before I can even think any further or ask the nurse, a team of doctors rushes towards me. I can gauge from their expressions and the frenetic activity around me that they haven't anticipated the situation they now find themselves in. A senior doctor checks my pulse, my pupils and my oxygen levels.

'Hello, Ms Kashyap. Can you hear me?' the doctor asks.

I try to speak, but can barely utter a word. It seems my vocal cords have been damaged. I simply nod to convey that I can hear him. He nods in return and the nurse standing beside him notes something in the patient file. I can sense the tension in his voice reduce a bit as he talks to the nurse. Though I am not able to hear them clearly, I can gauge it must be something about my condition. A series of questions follows—how am I feeling, do I know where I am, am I feeling any pain, am I able to move my body? In spite of failing in my initial attempts to speak, I manage to utter a word or two. I speak in a muffled tone but it is still clear enough for the others to understand. Once the doctor is done, he turns to the nurse. 'Vitals?' he asks her.

'Stable, sir,' she says, after checking the readings on the machine.

A smile of satisfaction appears on the doctor's face. 'Do you remember what happened to you and why you are here?' he asks.

As I shake my head, I can see his smile disappear. He speaks in low tones with his colleagues. Trying his best to hide his concern, he says to me, 'Do not worry, take some rest.'

I nod. I am tired and confused.

After everyone leaves the room, I make another attempt to recall the past that has led me to this point. As I struggle to remember, frustration hits me hard. Apprehension and several questions are running through my mind, and a tsunami of emotions has engulfed me. My body feels as if it is in a storm waiting for peace.

A little later, the door slides open again and a woman in her forties walks briskly towards me.

'Nandini ...' she says with a wide smile.

As she holds my hand, tears roll down her cheeks. I remain in a daze and stare at her from top to bottom. She is wearing a salwar suit and has a wedding ring on her hand. Neither her face nor the name she has uttered is familiar.

Nandini? The doctor had addressed me as Ms Kashyap. So, is my name Nandini Kashyap? I try desperately to remember but I have no memory at all. I look at her curiously.

'I am so happy today. I thought I'd lost you too,' she says as she runs her fingers through my hair. I can feel the warmth in her touch, but my mind stays on the words she had spoken.

Lost me too? Did she mean she had lost someone else? But who? And who is she?

I stare at her blankly. She seems to understand the conflict within my heart. Maybe the doctors have informed her about my memory or perhaps the confusion on my face has revealed that I cannot recognise her.

'I am your Maasi,' she says, stroking my face gently. 'Don't be tense. I know you are confused.' Then she takes a deep breath and reveals, 'You had a car accident, but you are okay. I don't wish to overwhelm you with all the details, but now that you are out of coma everything will be fine soon.'

Coma? The word hits me hard. The chaos in my head creates a sense of panic and chokes my brain. A shiver runs through my body. At least, that clarifies why I was bedridden and couldn't recall anything from my past. Have I lost my memory? How long have I been in this state? I feel lost. I want to melt into a puddle. I want to fall onto the street and let the wind push me far, far away. I want to dissolve in the storm that has hit me. I want to disappear.

'How long have I been here?' I ask her.

'Fourteen months. When you slipped into a coma, the doctors said that there was barely any chance that you would come back. But now you will soon recover and live a normal life again.'

Normal life? Was it really possible? Everything looks so scary. Especially as I remember nothing about my previous life, not even my own identity.

Who was I? Where were my parents? Where did I live? What did I do before my accident?

I can remember nothing. I can't even be sure that the lady in front of me is telling the truth. But I have no option other than believing her. I feel like just another lost soul floating helplessly with no control in the calm ocean of life. I'll go wherever the tide tells me to because I have no choice. Everything looks pointless, so why bother to fight?

2

My New Family

After four months of intensive physiotherapy, I feel good enough to climb a mountain. But mentally, even after multiple sessions with a psychologist, I am still recovering. I get nightmares in which I find myself struggling to breathe. Loud noises startle me and the stress of not knowing who I am is taking a toll on me. The thought of starting a new life is scary. The doctors are saying that I will take time to adjust to normal life again, that it is time now for me to go home. But I have no memories of my home. Everyone at the hospital is glad I am alive, though I have no feelings about it myself.

'Nandini, how are you feeling?' Maasi asks me today.

She is the only one who has visited me almost every day since I woke up after the accident. Though Maasi often mentions her daughter and husband, neither of them has visited me yet. But it doesn't matter.

'You look much better than the first day I saw you. How do you feel?' Maasi proudly pats my back, as if I have won an

Olympic medal. Just like our first meeting in the hospital, she has the same warmth in her touch and fondness in her eyes. By now, I know a few things about her. Her name is Usha Soni, she has been married for twenty years. I'll turn nineteen this year, and although she doesn't look it, her daughter is my age.

'I am good,' I answer every time. But I know I am not at all good. It's partly because she feels like a stranger. No matter how much affection she shows me, I feel nothing towards her.

One thing she still hasn't told me about is my parents. Where are they? When she said ... *lost you too* at our first meeting, did she mean my mother *had* died in the accident? Or had it been my father? Or had they both died much before my accident and I have always lived with Maasi and her family? Whenever I have tried to ask her, she has smiled and ignored my questions. She says that our families were close. But if that's true, why don't I get a sense of familiarity when we are together? Why don't my uncle and cousin visit me? Why doesn't Maasi reveal anything about them? It makes me uncomfortable, but I keep my thoughts to myself.

'I have completed all the formalities. It's time to go home,' she says. She picks up my bag and gets up excitedly to finally take me back.

I nod and walk out of the hospital with her, after thanking the staff who have given me a second life. As we walk, I turn towards Maasi who has a smile on her face. I don't know if I am happy or confused or dead inside, but I am convincing myself that from here on I'll be staying with her in the outskirts of Kangra town in Himachal Pradesh. Throughout the car ride, I keep looking outside trying to remember the place. But the sights, the sounds, the smells and everything around me, even though serene, are unknown. There is something mystical about the place and I feel uneasy. The sky, punched with clouds stretching across it, seems to be falling apart on me. I can smell the meadows as we pass through, but I cannot bring myself to appreciate them. The meadows look like a hideaway of the lost heaven where I have been trying to find my soul. I am sure anyone else would revel in the sense of inner peace and harmony the place invokes. But to me, each passing street looks like a puzzle that refuses to get solved. The grass is partying with the wind, dancing to its own rhythm. The trees seem like silhouettes in the glorious expanse. It is as if God is shouting at me to forget whatever has happened and open myself up to the new life that lies ahead of me.

After an hour-long drive, we arrive at Maasi's house. The bungalow is one of the many that stand beside each other on the lane. It has a small garden decorated with flower beds, and is well-maintained and clean. Looking at the doors, the walls and the paint, you know you are in a hill station. My eyes search for my sister and uncle as I enter the house but there is no one there. The house is silent. After showing me around, Maasi asks me to freshen up in my room while she makes tea.

'Where's everyone?' I ask. I am eager to meet them. I would think that they didn't exist if I hadn't seen their pictures in the living room. There are pictures of a few others too—of the family, I assume—and I try to guess if my mother is one of them. I want to ask Maasi but don't.

'They are on their way home. Your uncle had to complete some formalities for Rashi at her college. They should be back soon.'

I smile.

'Why don't you freshen up till then?' Maasi says. I can see she is doing her best to make me feel comfortable. She turns to enter the kitchen but instead walks towards me and makes me sit on the sofa.

'Listen, Nandini. I know all this feels new to you but, trust me, you will soon live a normal life again. We are with you.' She pauses for a while and then says, 'I am there for you. Always.'

'Thank you, Maasi,' I say with a shrug, the words unfamiliar to my tongue.

She smiles and holds my hand. I stare at our intertwined fingers, trying to remember at least something about my life. But there is nothing there. 'Promise me, if you remember anything about your past, you will first tell me.' Maasi's words shake me out of my thoughts and bring me back to reality.

'I will,' I say.

For the past four months, I have been floating along with the tide, letting it take me wherever it wants to go. I do what I'm told without questioning. I don't feel like going against the tide—that requires strength I don't have. Along with my memories, the car accident has robbed me of my emotions and desires.

I leave the living room and walk towards the washroom. I lock the door and lean against it. My chest feels heavy. I don't know what to do. I splash some cold water on my face to calm myself down. Staring back at me in the mirror is a girl I cannot recognise.

'Do you think you'll be all right one day? Happy?' I ask myself.

I don't know but I think Maasi's family will guide you to your happiness, the girl in the mirror answers.

I hear some loud noises outside. So, I quickly wash my face and walk out towards my room. I stop to hear the conversation going on in the living room.

'I don't want you to create a scene or act immaturely when you meet Nandini. I hope you understand that. I have already had enough,' I hear Maasi say. I don't understand what is going on, and even though I can just step outside to see for myself, I want to first listen to whatever is happening. I peep to see a girl standing in front of Maasi. I assume she is Rashi. She looks as old as me. But her skin has a glow that mine doesn't, probably thanks to all the medical treatment I have had to go through. Even though she is petite, she has a statuesque figure which she is flaunting in denim shorts and a deep-neck top. More than her appearance, I try to read her mind through her posture. I am keen to know why Maasi is warning her against creating a scene. What had I done?

'I have also had enough. I don't want her to stay here,' Rashi yells, throwing her hands in the air. That is the first time I have heard her voice, and I don't like her tone at all.

When I had stepped into the house an hour earlier, I had accepted that this would be my home, like Maasi had said. That her family would be mine too. But now, before even meeting me, my sister has decided that she didn't want me there. What she says next comes as a shocker. 'Despite telling you to look for some hostel or youth care centre for her, you have brought her to our house. How could you do that? When so much has already happened?'

I can bring myself to hear no further, my ears still ringing with Rashi's last words. I know in that moment that a storm will soon break the tide I am on and eventually drown me.

Hostel? Youth care centre? Why? Am I an orphan ... am I an orphan?

Worse than feeling like an orphan is the feeling of not being able to remember anything about my parents. What did they look like? Where did we live? What had happened to them? It made me wonder if I had anyone in this world I could claim as my own. The ones left were fighting with each other—one for me and one against me.

Rashi has been speaking continuously while I have been lost in my thoughts. All I manage to catch are the words, 'Sorry, but I can't stand her.'

Maasi points a finger towards her and firmly states her decision, 'Look, she's my sister's daughter and I just can't leave her alone on her first day out of the hospital. She'll stay here for as long as she wants.'

Rashi again throws her hands in the air in disgust and sits down on the sofa, facing a man in his late forties who I assume is my uncle. While mother and daughter have been yelling at each other, he has stayed silent—as if he doesn't exist in the family scene, as if his opinion doesn't matter. Rashi looks at him and, seeing no reaction, her brown eyes widen in surprise.

'Papa, at least you say something. Didn't we discuss this before?' she screams.

'I have nothing to say.' He strides forward and taps the cigar he is smoking in the ashtray. It seems he prefers to not take any sides and has left it for the mother-daughter duo to decide. But his unwillingness to support me makes it clear that he too isn't really keen on having me in the house.

After a moment of silence, Maasi says to him, 'It's better you don't say anything. Because if I start speaking, you will not be able to handle it.'

There is something wrong with this family. It isn't just about me; I can clearly see that there is some tension between all of them. I want to know the reason. Why are their family dynamics so skewed? And why does Rashi dislike me so much?

I eventually step out of my room. Maasi sees me and freezes. She is clearly wondering if I overheard their conversation. The fear on her face gives her away. I shift my gaze from Maasi to the others. I debate whether I should simply leave. With all eyes on me, I feel an uncomfortable sensation that grows by the minute. The silence makes me feel that I should just go back to my room.

'Nandini ... meet Rashi and your uncle,' Maasi says with an uncomfortable smile.

I step closer to Rashi and look at her. The sense of awkwardness between us is palpable. Should I smile? Should I shake her hand or just say hello? What am I supposed to do?

I want to just run away, but the look of anticipation on Maasi's face stops me. Where would I run to anyway? It is not like I have a choice, I am a part of this family now.

'Hi ...' I say.

She doesn't say a word and forces herself to smile. The man who I guess I should call uncle flashes a smile in my direction too. Maasi watches our interaction closely.

'It's great to have you with us. How are you feeling now?' He steps forward, stretching out his hand towards me, intending to ruffle my hair. But I step back.

'Easy, Ravi,' Maasi says. 'Don't rush her.'

He withdraws his hand and sits at the dining table. Maasi has prepared snacks and tea for everyone.

'Nandini, take a seat. You must be hungry,' she says.

I pull a chair back and say, 'Thank you.'

I suddenly feel a hand above me. It is Rashi's.

'That's my chair. You can sit on the other one.'

She has an authoritative look on her face but Maasi isn't pleased with her attitude. 'What will happen if you sit on the other one, Rashi?'

Rashi retaliates with, 'What will happen if she sits on the other one?'

Before the fumes of anger can suffocate everyone in the room, I quietly answer, 'It's okay. I'll take the other one.'

We eat the kebabs that Maasi has cooked. However, sitting on that dining table watching everyone, I cannot help but feel like an outsider intruding on their family. And that brings me back to that one question that I have been pondering over in my head, again and again, ever since I have woken up from my coma.

Where is my real family?

That night, as I sit alone in my room, my mind is at war. A battle between myself and the darkness is swirling around me. I look at myself in the mirror. My eyes look sunken and the long night dress hangs lifelessly against my ashen skin. The darkness has taken away my power to think. After staring at the ceiling fan for what seems like an eternity, I switch on the television. I browse through the channels and stop at a news channel. I can remember the general details of what is being shown—a follow-up on the terrorist attack that had happened some time ago—but I cannot recollect anything else about my past. After a while, I hear a knock on my door and Maasi enters my room.

I suddenly feel nervous and cannot help but think that she has come to tell me something urgently. Strange thoughts of her asking me to leave her house crowd my mind. She certainly looks upset because of the incident in the evening and her next—defensive—words confirm that.

'Are you upset with what happened at the dining table?' she asks, sitting close to me. I find her presence reassuring. Maybe because she is the only one who cares about me and has stood up for me. At least it seems that way.

'No, I am not,' I lie. Even though I am upset, Maasi doesn't need to know that, or the reason why I am upset. She is oblivious to the fact that I had overheard their entire conversation earlier, and I don't enlighten her. Telling her would only trouble her more. I know she is asking me about Rashi's rude behaviour towards me. 'I mean, I wasn't expecting her to be rude and, thus, was shocked initially. But now I am fine,' I pretend.

She smiles at me. I guess she only wanted to know if I'd overheard the living room conversation between her, Rashi and uncle, before I had entered the room. She looks relieved, believing what I said. She takes a deep breath and says, 'You know, she's really a pampered child and has never shared her space with anyone.' She is clearly defending Rashi so that I don't hold any grudges against her. After all, we are sisters and now have to live under the same roof. 'It's not only about you; even with us her behaviour is sometimes erratic. My parents used to tell me to have another child so that she'd get used to sharing her things from childhood. That never happened.'

Maasi then moves on, trying to jog my memories. According to her, Rashi and I had shared a good bond prior to my accident, and even when we had been kids and our families had gone out on outings, we had loved each other's company. I don't know whether to believe her or not, because after what I experienced today, it looks like she is simply covering up for Rashi. Anyway, I don't argue with her and just nod. She gets up to leave and I finally ask her what I have wanted to all along. 'Maasi ...' She stops, looks back and waits for me to say more. 'Where are my mom and dad?' I ask her calmly.

The silence that follows makes me extremely uncomfortable. Finally, she says, 'Not now, Nandini. I'll tell you at the right time.'

I hadn't expected her to say that. Is she hiding something from me? And if so, why? It seems like whatever happened a year ago didn't just hurt me, but also the people around me.

'Are they dead?' I ask her directly.

She turns her eyes away from me. The only visible reaction I see are her hands clenching tightly. Looks like the suspicion I have been harbouring for months is true. Before I can probe further, she repeats, 'Not now, Nandini. Trust me, I will tell you everything. But now is not the time.' The agitation within her is visible on her face. Still, she somehow manages to look into my eyes and adds, 'Believe me.'

'I trust you,' I say.

I think to myself: *It's always harder to be the one left behind. Her sister and brother-in-law's deaths must have been hard on Maasi. Much worse than seeing me in a coma for a year.* I did trust her. I just prayed that she wouldn't break it.

3

Usha Soni: I'll Protect Nandini

It has been very disconcerting for Rashi to have Nandini enter our life. For the last year or so, our routine had been consistent. Every morning, I would first ensure that Rashi went to college on time and then cook lunch for Anil. After that, I would go to work at my beauty parlour. In the evenings, I would make sure to reach the hospital by the time the doctors came for their rounds to check up on Nandini. By the time I would reach home, Rashi would be back from college, followed soon after by Anil. After dinner, we'd watch some television together before calling it a day. Interspersed in our everyday life were regular arguments about not bringing Nandini home—reasons for which would never surface in our conversations but were known to each of us.

The same argument would have turned nasty in Nandini's presence, but before things got out of control, I had taken charge of the situation. Luckily, she had been in her room at that time and hadn't heard anything. I had still wanted to make sure of that and had decided to talk with her. I wanted to gauge how much she knew based on her response to Rashi's treatment of her.

Before going to Nandini's room last night, I had gone to the storeroom to open one of the boxes that contained Nandini's belongings, which I'd got from didi's home after the accident. Nandini had had most of her important things like her mobile, laptop and identity cards with her when the car had crashed. The police had handed them over to me at the hospital. I had kept all that in the box along with her other personal things.

As I had pulled back the brown tape on the box—the noise screeching through the silence of the store room—and lifted the cardboard flaps, it had felt as if old wounds that I'd attempted to stitch up were reopening. My fingers had drifted along the photo frames kept inside—moments of perfection captured for an eternity that were now clinging to me like unbearable objects. Didi's face had appeared before me. I had felt guilty looking at her picture because I still hadn't disclosed everything to Nandini. I had quickly retaped the box and slid it back into its original place. I hadn't been ready for Nandini's questions just then. I had kept my thoughts to myself for so long that I was scared about what would happen when they eventually erupted.

Even though I have been running away from her questions for a long time, last night Nandini eventually asked the dreaded question.

Are they dead?

I had felt so alone in that moment even though my family was all around me. I had somehow managed to convince her that I would reveal everything to her soon. She agreed but I could sense that she wasn't really satisfied. She had known that it wasn't about her, but about me. I just hadn't been ready .

I could hardly sleep last night. Today morning, after making breakfast and packing Anil's lunchbox, I took my blood pressure tablet and went to sit on the daybed in the porch. I have decided to spend time with Nandini and take her out to make her feel better. Pursing my lips, I pull out my phone and type out a quick excuse to the head beautician of the parlour.

'Good morning.'

I look up from my phone to see Nandini smiling down at me, the sun behind her plunging her into a dark silhouette.

'Good morning,' I greet her and say, 'I hope you slept well.'

She nods and says, 'Much better than the hospital.'

I smile and say, 'I understand how that feels,' even though I'm fully aware that I have no idea how it must feel to be in her place. God has been entirely unfair to this young girl this past year. And yet, she has a smile on her face. Although I know a lot of pain is hidden behind it, I'm impressed she still has the strength to live another day.

'Uncle's ready for office?' she asks. I assume she just wants to say something to me, and isn't really interested in her uncle's whereabouts.

'Yes, come along.'

I pull myself up from the daybed and start towards the kitchen, when Rashi's ringing phone catches my attention. She is in the washroom and must have left her phone on the dining table. Usually, she never lets her phone out of her sight and hates it if anyone comes between them. But the nonstop ringtone forces me to check it. The person calling finally gives up and sends Rashi a message. It is from a boy named Sahil.

Chill. She's just your sister. The message stays on the display screen for a bit.

Curious, I give into temptation. I click on the WhatsApp icon to see the original message Rashi must have sent, which Sahil has replied to.

My sister is now staying with us. I just wish she would run away from this house.

I scroll up but that is the only message concerning Nandini. It makes me furious. I look up and see Nandini staring blankly at me. I'm sure she knows I have seen something that I shouldn't have. I decide to speak with Rashi openly about it later, but for now I leave the phone exactly where I found it.

'Nandini, can you bring me the coffee kept in the kitchen?' I tell her as I sit on the chair.

'Mummy, I want a thousand rupees.' Rashi appears in front of me carrying her college bag. I can read her eyes. Last night's tussle is still on her mind.

'Why? Anything special today?' I ask, taking the glass of coffee from Nandini's hand. Rashi runs her eyes over Nandini for a few seconds, before looking back at me and asking, 'Now I can't even ask for money from my own mother? Does it require a special occasion?'

There is a long, excruciating pause. I can sense the displeasure in the air mixing with the rich scent of coffee. I raise my eyebrows, surprised with her answer.

'I just want to know why you need the money. That's it.'

I get up from my chair and bring the cash from the bedroom.

'Don't be late in the evening,' I say before handing the money to her.

Her phone rings, as she wears her sandals and opens the door, giving Nandini a moment to bid her goodbye. 'Bye, have a nice day.'

But Rashi just gives her a sly smile and leaves without saying a word. Nandini must have surely felt uncomfortable by her gesture. To make light of the situation, I laugh and say, 'Kids these days ... are tough to handle.'

I take the coffee mug in my hand and look at the steam rising from it—the swirling patterns mixing with the dust particles are almost hypnotic. I take a breath to calm myself. 'Nandini, make yourself comfortable. Breakfast is on the table.'

I take Anil's lunchbox to the bedroom to give it to him. He is buttoning his shirt when he sees me walking inside and says, 'Usha, we need to talk.' He averts his gaze and takes the tiffin box from my hand.

'About what?' I ask.

'Nandini.'

'Anil ...' I let out a long, deep sigh. 'Not now, please.'

I follow him with my eyes, but before I can say anything else, he walks out. I shake my head, hoping to get rid of my thoughts, and go back to Nandini. She has been a silent observer of everything that has happened in the house since morning. I wonder if she feels at home here. However, whether she feels it or not, we are her only family.

4

Nandini: Back to Normal Life?

I had thought Maasi and her family would be the lighthouse that would guide me back to happiness but I had been wrong. They weren't as welcoming as I had thought they would be. And though Maasi supports me wholeheartedly, I still have a strong feeling that she is hiding something. Once Rashi leaves, I go back to my room and hide under the fuzzy blanket, trying to find the purpose of my life while I drink coffee. After some time, I grudgingly swap the blanket with my jacket and open the bedroom door to see Maasi waiting for me.

'You aren't ready yet?' she says, the corner of her lips turning up at my perplexed expression.

'Were we supposed to go somewhere?' I step back and adjust my jacket.

'I had planned to take you out to see the town.' Maasi flashes a smile.

I ask her to give me some time to get ready. We go to the nearby market, and then to her beauty parlour. It is a small one but seems popular, looking at the number of people inside. She says she wants me to get familiar with the town.

Over the next few weeks, we go to several nearby places. It takes me time to adjust to the unfamiliar territory—new roads, new shops, new neighbours—but eventually I accept that this is going to be my new normal life. More than anything else, I have gotten used to the environment at home. I occasionally talk to Rashi, but she rarely starts a conversation with me. Initially, it would affect me but now I have given up trying to be friendly towards her. Since the first day we met, Uncle has only spoken to me when necessary, and it has stayed that way. However, in the few conversations we have had, he has made sure to include me and has treated me well. I can feel as if some tension has arisen between Maasi and him, but I don't know the reason for it. And I don't really bother about it either, because in all these weeks, Maasi has been the one who has made me feel comfortable in this home. I don't want to pry into her life.

There are some days, when I still get nightmares of being trapped in the hospital, of my body being glued to the bed, of being unable to move. I usually wake up from these in terror and sweat.

In this manner, time has passed by, and seasons have changed. Today, it is yet another day of Kangra being surrounded by dark clouds. I try to enjoy the weather by opening the windows of my room. Thunderstorms don't scare me as much as my nightmares. The lush, green mountains and the sound of raindrops actually make me feel better. I take the juice bottle that Maasi has kept on the table for me and settle down next to the window for an evening of staring vacantly at nature outside. One of the benefits of Maasi's house is that it is on the far end of a road that is devoid of any traffic. I am reading a book when Maasi comes inside with a file and a box sealed with brown tape. She gives me a pleasant smile, but my attention is on the file she holds.

'Nandini,' she says in a serious tone and sits on the bed in front of me, 'I want to talk to you.'

The intensity in her voice scares me, making me wonder if I have done anything to upset her. But I brush off my worries and say, 'Sure.'

She winces, searching for the right words. 'I don't know if you will take what I say positively, but I want you to.'

I brace myself for the worst. 'Nandini, you need to join college again,' she says.

I absorb this information, but don't say anything immediately. *College?* I think. Maasi's hopeful eyes want me to accept what she is saying as it is, but when I just stare at her blankly, she puts more force in her request.

'Look, you can surely join college again. Remember the tests we got done last week on the doctor's suggestion?' she asks. I nod. 'The results came earlier today and on the way home, I met the doctor too.'

I raise my eyebrows, curious to know my progress. 'He said that you are going through retrograde memory loss. That means your mind is unconsciously suppressing your memories but your general knowledge is intact. Touchwood,' she adds, while knocking the wooden headboard of the bed.

I remain silent, not knowing how to react. I have just started being able to relax in this house after so many weeks and suddenly I am being asked to leave my comfort zone again.

What if I am not able to handle the pressures of college? I was in a coma for a year, and I'm sure, at this moment, I am far behind my peers academically.

'We are not sure whether your memories will even return, but I don't want you to lose the opportunities ahead of you. Staying at home won't help you either,' Maasi continues with her justifications.

'Do you think I can keep up with others?' I ask, still not sure if it is the right decision.

'I know you can. You can restart the first year of BA. It's time for you to go out, meet new friends and create your identity again. I know it will be hard in the beginning—catching up on studies and getting yourself composed mentally—but I really want you to get back to how you were before the accident.'

Her words are comforting and reassure me, but I am afraid. However, I cannot deny that a part of me is also thrilled about the prospect of finally having a life outside of home.

I decide to give it a try. 'Okay, if you say so.'

Maasi's face lights up. 'That's awesome. I am proud of you.'

She hands over the brown-taped box to me and says that it contains a few things that used to belong to me. Nandini of a few weeks ago would have jumped to open the box right then and there, but today's Nandini doesn't do that. A sensation of bubbling excitement is washing over my body. I am keener to paint my future rather than dig into my past that lies in the box. I see Maasi punching some numbers on her phone. I move closer to her and say, 'Thanks.' This feeling of gentle happiness has brought butterflies to my stomach. I look at Maasi, the one who is doing everything possible to give me a good life, and add, 'For taking care of me, and doing everything for me.'

She smiles and says, 'You don't need to thank me. Remember, if you ever need to talk to someone, I am always there.'

After completing the formalities over the next few days, my admission in the first year of RS College is confirmed. I'm told I can start a week later.

Maasi drives me to college on the first day. As expected, Rashi refuses to come along. Not that Maasi wants me to go alone with her, but I had thought that the half-hour drive could have been an icebreaker between us. After all, she is my senior in college now. As we get closer, I can feel my heart beating faster and my mouth turning dry. I had been thrilled when I'd first made the decision to re-join college. But today I was feeling extremely nervous. How would college be? Would I like the people around me? Ever since I woke up in the hospital, I have confined myself to a small space, with no one to answer to and no one to invade my mind. But that is all going to change now. My actions will no longer go unnoticed. Maasi sees me nervously shifting my gaze and tapping my legs continuously. She gives me an encouraging smile and says, 'Are you nervous? Don't worry.'

I fake a smile to show her I am not worried, but even I am not convinced with it. Despite several attempts, I haven't been able to brush off the jitters. We eventually arrive at the college and a volcano of questions again erupts in my mind.

People will surely question the reason behind my transfer from another college. If I refuse to answer, will they judge me and talk behind my back? What if they come to know my medical history?

It's not something I am deliberately hiding because I am embarrassed; I just don't want any unnecessary attention on myself again.

'We have reached. You want me to come along with you to the office?' Maasi's words jolt my train of thought.

'No, I'll manage,' I say. I don't want to attract curious eyes, which is bound to happen if my guardian accompanies me inside. I step out of the car and look at the college building in front of me. I am standing in front of a huge gate and the campus beyond it looks unbelievably large. It is time to get used to my new life, I tell myself. I turn around to bid Maasi goodbye.

'Okay, all the best,' she says as I walk away from the car.

I see a few students with books in their hands, a few sitting on the benches at the edge of the campus and a few just chitchatting with each other. I take a deep breath and relax a bit. Suddenly, I hear a voice behind me, 'Hey.' I turn around to see a stylish boy who has long hair and a beard that suits him well. I look at him, wondering what he was going to say next. I wish I could just walk away or pretend that I was getting a phone call. That way I wouldn't have to speak to him. It isn't anything about him—it is all me. I wasn't expecting anyone to talk to me so soon after entering the college. When I don't respond, he says, 'Looking for something? You seem to be lost.' He flashes a crooked smile at me.

I wish I could get lost. I raise my eyebrows slightly.

'Oh ya,' is all I manage to say. I look down at the photograph of the college timetable on my phone, increasingly aware of my rising body temperature. Without looking up, I say, 'I was looking for my classroom.'

'New admission?' he asks as I squeeze past him towards the corridor. 'I'll help you.'

'Sure,' I reply, my legs refusing to move. I don't think I have made a good first impression and curse myself under my breath. He takes a couple of steps and is beside me again. 'Oh, before I forget, I am Rudra.'

He flashes me a breath-taking smile and I find my words getting stuck in my throat.

'Nandini,' I answer. 'It's my first day here today and, to be honest, I am a little lost looking for my class,' I admit. I like the answer I give him this time.

'I'll help you,' he repeats, leaning in to have a look at the timetable on my phone. 'What's your classroom number?'

'Room number five. Any idea where that is?' I ask.

'Of course, it's on the first floor,' he answers. 'I am also going upstairs. Come along.'

My lips tighten and, for a moment, I expect myself to tell him that I'd manage on my own. But, instead, I smile and say, 'Sure.'

He leads the way and, though I don't intend to, I walk along with him through the corridor. All the while, I say nothing, keeping my eyes on the people around me and on the college walls which sport beautiful artwork and motivational quotes. I, suddenly, realise that he has slowed his pace and I turn to him to see what has happened. He is smiling at a guy, maybe his friend, who is walking towards us.

'Hey, Sahil,' Rudra says and clasps the other boy's shoulder. They both sport a similar beard and are of the same height—much taller than me. But Sahil is even better-looking than Rudra, who asks him, 'How come you are in college for the first lecture?'

'I had to submit the assignment before class. You know how *Chaman* would react if I don't,' he grins. His smile is mischievous but innocent.

He soon realises that I am standing next to Rudra and our eyes meet. His eyes are as deep as they are expressive, and I feel I might get lost in them if I continue staring at him. He is handsome—perhaps not in the conventional sense but he would stand out in a crowd. He stares right back at me and I feel uneasy. As if I am not supposed to be here. I can see a hint of pain in his eyes, which disappears as suddenly as it had emerged. It seems like he wasn't expecting to see me here. But I have never met Sahil before, so what can that look mean?

His next question to Rudra, whispered loud enough, confirms my suspicions. 'Where did you meet her and why are you with her?'

'She's a new admission.' Rudra turns his head towards me, 'Sahil, meet Nandini. Nandini, meet Sahil.' He introduces us formally, not noticing that our staring game is still going on.

Sahil? I don't think I have ever heard that name before. *Why does he look so angry with me?* I think.

I ignore his stares and greet him, 'Hello.'

He looks at me as if he wants to say something. But he doesn't.

'Anyway, Nandini, let's leave.' Rudra interrupts and finally ends our staring game. 'Sahil, I'll catch you later.'

Who was he? Does he know who I am? I ask myself as I walk silently behind Rudra. I cannot help turning back quickly. And as expected, Sahil is still there. He hasn't moved from his spot and is still watching me.

Rudra shows me to my classroom and then walks towards his, which is on the other side of the floor. I check the time on my watch; my lecture doesn't start for another fifteen minutes. I decide to stroll around to avoid any unnecessary conversations with my classmates. Walking around aimlessly, I reach the other end of the floor. I turn around to walk back to my classroom and see Sahil leaning against the wall a few metres away. Maybe he is waiting for someone else. But when he doesn't move, I know he is there for me. All of a sudden, he is towering in front of me and my body starts to feel numb. Unexpectedly, he pushes me inside one of the empty classrooms; the raging, intimidating look in his eyes scares me and all I can do is to stare back at him.

'Sahil? What are you doing?' I whisper. I hug my bag to my chest, trying to calm myself down.

'What are *you* doing here?' he asks in an authoritative tone, as if I am someone he knows closely.

I am baffled by his question and want to run away from him. Instead, I say, 'I am waiting for my lectures to begin.'

I really should have just spoken to my new classmates instead of getting caught here with Sahil.

'Are you trying to be smart with me?' He shushes me and continues, 'What are you doing in my college? And why are you a junior?

Does he really know me? Is it possible that we knew each other before my accident? I do not know how to react.

'I am sorry but do I know you?'

He laughs at my question. 'Wow, really? You don't know me?' He takes a step back and looks at me from head to toe. He ruffles his hair in anger. 'You're pretending to be Rudra's good friend and now you're saying that you don't know me?'

'I don't ...' I wave my hand in the air and with wide eyes full of panic and confusion, I say, 'Please, I am not lying ... let me clarify.'

'Stop acting, Nandini. If you really want to pretend like you don't know me, it is fine. I'll pretend not to know you either.'

'Wait, I am not pretending.' I try to clarify but he thinks I am lying. With a look of pure disgust, he pushes himself away from me and walks out of the classroom.

What just happened here? Why did he get so mad at me? What had I done wrong? I have no answers.

5

Nandini: Who Is He?

The only certain thing about life is uncertainty, I know that. In the evening, as I sit to think about how I could be associated with Sahil, nothing comes to mind. When Maasi had asked me earlier how my first day back in college had been, I'd faked a smile and said that it had been refreshing. Truth be told, keeping aside my encounter with Sahil, even being surrounded by so many people had discomfited me, made me claustrophobic. I had kept to myself between the lectures because I'd needed time to process what the professors were teaching. Though my general knowledge was intact, the lectures felt torturous to a rusted brain that was wired to sleep through the day. If I had told Maasi the truth about my day, she would have panicked. That was my second lie of the day. The first had come when my classmates had bombarded me with questions about myself. *Where was I from? Why did I leave Khajjiar and shift to Kangra? Why hadn't I attended college from the first day of the term?*

I had known that everyone would ask me for all these details, so Maasi had instructed me today morning to tell everyone that I wasn't comfortable sharing my medical condition. She had asked me to say that my parents had shifted to the US as my father hadn't wanted to miss out on a good opportunity. I was to tell them that instead of going along with them, I had decided to finish my studies in Kangra. I had repeated this story again and again, and my classmates had seemed convinced. In college, I had even tried to spot Rashi but hadn't been able to. Rashi had driven to college and back on her two-wheeler, while Maasi had dropped and picked me up.

The next day, the walk to the classroom feels familiar. I am about to climb the stairs when I see Rudra. He has the same charming smile on his face.

'Hi,' he greets me. I smile back at him, adjusting my bag on my shoulder.

'So, how was your first day?' he asks. I was sure if I gave him a detailed response, he would next ask me for my phone number. So, I keep it short and simple, 'Nice.'

'How about a coffee in the canteen right now? We still have time.'

There he goes, I say in my mind. When I don't reply, he says, 'You'll get one of the best coffees in our canteen. Kangra's best.'

Rudra is clearly a popular boy. Everyone who walks past us greets him with a smile, including the girls. But for some reason, he wants to have coffee with me—a girl nobody knows, not even she herself.

'Maybe some other time,' I say, trying to avoid him, 'I need to go to the library right now.'

'No problem.' He moves to make way for me. As I am about to enter the library, I bump into Sahil again.

'Really? Once again?' He looks appalled to see me. I cannot control myself and ask, 'What have I done that you are so mad at me?'

He looks at me in disbelief, 'You know the answer to that, don't you? Or do you still want to pretend you don't remember what you did to me and what happened between us?'

'No, I don't remember. What did I do to you?' I answer honestly. He shakes his head and almost screams back at me, 'You are a genius, Ms Nandini Kashyap.' He takes a step closer and I can feel his breath on my face. 'I really don't know what you are up to. A year ago, you maliciously dumped me by way of a text message and now you are back only to pretend you know nothing about me. Nothing about us!'

I am dumbfounded. Is that what I had really done? I can finally understand the reason behind his rage. But is he telling the truth or making up a story?

'I really don't remember anything, Sahil. You need to listen to me,' I say. However, even though I say this, I am not sure I am ready to reveal to him that I have lost my memory. He doesn't complicate the situation for me, and just slings his bag on his shoulders and says, 'Forget it. I don't give a damn. Just stay the fuck away from me.'

He steps away and walks downstairs when I see Rashi coming up. I thank God that she hadn't seen me with Sahil or overheard our conversation. She would have surely created a fuss. But she doesn't notice me at all. She comes up to Sahil, puts her arms around him and starts walking away with him.

'What took you so long ...?' I hear her say as they turn into a corner, out of sight.

Is Rashi his new girlfriend? Had Sahil and I really been in a relationship in the past? Guilt rams into me hard. I want to know if he is telling the truth, but I have no way of confirming what he has told me.

It is only when I return home and am pacing the room, not being able to comprehend all that had happened in college, that I remember the brown-taped box Maasi had given me. She had said that it contained my belongings, including my laptop and old mobile. I had placed it under the bed and forgotten all about it, convinced I needed to focus on the future and not the past. Without wasting another second, I reach down for the box, pull it out and tear it apart. The first thing I see is a photo of me smiling standing next to an unfamiliar woman. My face resembles hers and I assume she must be my mother. I flip through a few more photographs, but even then my memories don't get triggered and I feel nothing. I keep the photographs aside and reach for the laptop and mobile. I hope they are in working condition. After charging both for some time, I can switch on at least my phone.

If Sahil and I were somehow connected in the past, I'll definitely find something on my phone. If Sahil was telling the truth, I'll surely get to know. I find his number saved in my contact list. In my inbox are several text conversations with Sahil.

He hadn't been lying. We had been in a relationship. My photo gallery has a separate folder called 'My love'. I swipe through a few of the photographs but I don't remember where the photos had been clicked. I can tell the location isn't Kangra. These photos of Sahil and me speak a thousand words and all say one thing: we had loved each other. I keep the phone aside and let out a painful sigh. People say that whatever happens, happens for a reason. In my case, the reason is immaterial; I cannot even recollect what had happened between us. I want the floor to swallow me up whole. If someone had asked me when I'd first arrived at Maasi's place about the specific things I wasn't looking for, the top two would have been love and enemies. *Well done, Nandini, expertly executed. Now you have an ex-boyfriend and a sister who hates you.* I shake my head, hoping to dislodge the discomfiting memory of our encounter. But I cannot.

Sahil used to be so madly in love with me. Then why did I dump him? And how was I going to survive college not knowing that?

6

Nandini: Love or Courtesy?

The next few days are full of mixed emotions. On the one hand, I am trying to concentrate on my studies. But on the other, it has become almost impossible to avoid bumping into Sahil whenever we are both in college—sometimes it's at the library, sometimes near the canteen and sometimes when he is with Rudra, who often gives me a friendly wave. Although I usually avoid waving back and acknowledge Rudra only with a slight smile, that is enough to anger Sahil even more. Even though we never speak to each other, I can see pain in his eyes. As guilty as I feel, I don't know what to say to him. He is unwilling to listen to me.

And if that isn't enough, Rashi makes the whole situation worse. She can sense the discomfort between Sahil and me. I had initially thought that she hadn't noticed my presence when I had first encountered Sahil. But I later learn that she avoids me intentionally and notices that Sahil always becomes tense in my presence. I only realise this when she loses her temper one day. We are alone at home and I am looking for something to eat in the fridge, when she shoves at the door as if it were a punching bag and says, 'I know what you are trying to do.' She is bubbling with anger.

'What do you mean?' I reply calmly and open the fridge door again.

She probably thinks it is a retaliatory act on my part, and shoves the door harder this time. I don't try to open it again and cross my arms.

'I am warning you to stay away from Sahil.'

I don't respond and go back to my room. It is better to stay away from this conversation. Anyway, I hardly interact with either of them in college. The good thing is that my initial jitters about adjusting to college life again and being surrounded by so many people has vanished. Maybe because people don't know the truth about me and cannot gossip about me, nobody bothers with me. Apart from a few classmates, I barely speak to anyone. I am happy in my own space. Moreover, Maasi has stopped dropping me to college as even she feels I can now manage on my own.

One day, I am waiting at my bus stop for a bus to come along since I have missed my regular bus to college.

'What's taking this bus so long?' I say out loud to no one.

A girl who is standing beside me hears it and turns towards me. She smiles endearingly and responds, 'It says it's just two minutes away.'

The girl has a crutch under her left armpit. My gaze instinctively shifts to her left leg and I see it is weaker than the other. For a moment, I want to sympathise with her but that thought vanishes as soon as I realise she doesn't need my pity.

She seems perfectly independent and is waiting for a bus at the stop just as I am.

I lift my head and look back at her. Her skin is glowing in the bright sunlight. She has striking features and a charming face.

'What are you talking about?' I ask.

'Don't you have the app?'

'Which app?' I question, narrowing my eyes.

'Let me see your phone.'

I hesitate for a second; after all she is a stranger. But then what she says makes me feel silly. 'Don't worry, I can't run away with your phone even if I want to.' She lifts her crutch and laughs.

Chagrined, I purse my lips and hand over the phone.

'It's called HP Transport. You can get real-time status updates about your bus.' She finds the app and hands my phone back to me.

I thank her, and she turns around and starts listening to music. Minutes later, the bus arrives. Everyone allows her to board first.

'May I help you?' I ask, stepping forward to lend a hand.

'Oh. Because of this?' She laughs. 'I am good; this is routine and I am used to it.' She puts her right foot on the first step and drags the other one inside with ease. 'I specifically take this bus because it has a lower floor.'

I feel an instant connection with her. I don't know if it is because she is disabled or because she has willingly helped me, but I love her energy. The bus is crowded—bags are pressed against butts and feet are searching for empty spaces on the bus floor. I manage to snake my way to the reserved seats for disabled passengers along with her. She has barely taken her seat when the bus jerks forward. Her ID badge falls off her lap. I bend down to pick it up for her.

'Oh, you are also from my college. Second year. I've never seen you?' I say as I hand her badge back to her. She just looks up at me and thanks me. My question seems to have disturbed her. 'Sorry. I just meant I have not seen you at the bus stop before or on campus,' I say.

'Don't ask. It's a long story.' She glances at me for a second and then avoids eye contact with me by staring outside the bus. 'It's my first day today. If I could, I would have avoided attending college altogether.'

I don't want to probe into her personal life and simply brush off the topic. It's clear she wants that too because she asks me, 'You are in the first year?'

I nod.

'Great, so you can be my bus stop friend. And you have already seen my name on the badge. I am Megha,' she says with a laugh.

I realise I haven't introduced myself. I laugh back and say, 'I am Nandini.'

For the first time in a long time, I am having a conversation with someone who willingly wants to talk to me. It feels good to laugh. Our stop arrives and we get off. We both look sideways to cross the road safely. Megha is rambling on when, suddenly, I realise that my feet are refusing to move. Even after months of physiotherapy, its seems I haven't fully recovered. Megha who has already walked a few steps ahead of me turns back to see me staring blankly at the car racing towards me. But before she can shout, somebody else grabs my right arm and pulls me back. I turn to see who it is. And as soon as I realise who it is, I wish I can zone out again. His eyes carry their usual deep-rooted angst.

'Sahil,' I groan.

My heart starts beating faster. It isn't because I have just survived one more accident but because of the way Sahil is still looking at me. He has a tight grip on my arm as if he is afraid to lose me again. I can feel his breath on my cheeks and his strong CK perfume is hypnotising. The fragrance seems strangely familiar.

Sahil, instead of speaking to me, asks my travel companion, 'Are you fine, Megha?'

Still in his grip, I turn to look at her as she nods, equally shocked.

Before I can speak to him or thank him, his grip on me loosens, and he walks away without another word. I come back to my senses and step towards Megha.

'Are you okay? What happened to you?' she asks in concern.

'Don't ask, it's a long story.' I repeat her own words from earlier.

She laughs, but I have a poker face. I cannot stop thinking about Sahil. Had his action to save me arisen out of love and concern or just humanity? It is tough to make out. But whatever the reason, it has made me question my identity. I feel like a leaf which has been plucked from a tree's branch and dropped on the ground, only to be later blamed for falling. But the leaf is naïve just like me, not aware of anything that is happening around it, simply drifting along with the force of the wind.

7

Nandini: Trust Me, I Didn't Do It

I find it ironic that the people we meet by accident are often the ones who become one of the most important parts of our lives. *'I'll be your bus stop friend,'* Megha had said when we'd met for the first time. She had been right. Since then, not only have we come to college together in the same bus but we have also started hanging out together during breaks and after college. The limelight that I had been avoiding till now, was now again on me, because Megha is very popular. But I don't mind it this time because she is a strong person and appreciates that I don't judge or pity her for her condition.

'I love how you think I am a strong girl. Not that I need validation from you but coming from a friend, it means a lot,' Megha says.

She has this habit of rambling on even when I'm not paying attention, but I love being around her.

And I always frown when she says this. 'I don't do it just to come across as a noble person. I mean it; I really don't care what people think of you.'

This is one of the reasons she loves my company. And I feel as if she is the only friend I have, someone who I can trust. Yet, I still haven't revealed anything to her about my past. Whenever she asks me why I am a year behind my age in college, I lie about having dropped a year. But she doesn't seem too convinced and keeps doubting me.

'Are we going out today after college?' Megha asks one day as we are walking towards the college gate.

'Yes, sure,' I say. It is Monday and going out after college to a café has become our routine.

'Okay, then see you.'

She goes in the direction of her class and I walk towards mine. I attend all my lectures even though most of them are boring. I struggle with some subjects, but I'm getting better at others. During the break, when I come outside, I find Rashi waiting for me.

That's unexpected. What's she doing here? Rashi always ignores me during college hours; I doubt she has even told her friends that I am her sister. But I don't really care; it's not like she has ever treated me like one. So, what is the point of even acknowledging our relationship in college? Relationships should be felt, lived and nourished; it's a bond that needs to be built. If that's not the case, it's better to not fake it.

'What's the matter?' I ask her when I see that she isn't moving, but is smiling slyly at me.

'You didn't take my warning seriously, did you?' she asks.

I don't know what she is talking about because if it is about Sahil, I never speak to him, apart from that one time when he had saved me from the car accident.

'What are you saying?' I ask, glancing at the people around us to avoid looking into her eyes. That's when I see a few girls staring at me with scorn on their faces, and whispering something to each other.

'Sahil ...' She stress on his name, 'I told you to stay away from him. But you didn't. So, I have had to take charge. He is going to cut all ties with you. Brace yourself for what's coming your way.'

Without clarifying any more, she just turns and walks away. *What did Rashi mean? Brace myself?* I don't have to wait for too long for an answer. I see our head of department walking towards me. Before I can greet him, he orders in a stern voice, 'Ms Nandini Kashyap, I want you in my office right now.'

'Me?' I ask. *Why does he want to meet me? It must be a mistake.*

'Yes, you. I'll see you in five.'

Knowing that there was only one way to end this confusion, I briskly walk towards the corridor that leads to his cabin. I pass by a group of students and am so stunned by what I see that I freeze. Sprayed on the wall are the words: *Sahil Avasthi is a pimp – says Nandini Kashyap.*

This is a nightmare! I am praying that someone will shake me awake and tell me that this is a dream. I realise now what Rashi had meant when she had said she was taking charge. I am gobsmacked. It is like Rashi has pushed me into the bowels of hell and has left no way open for me to climb out.

How could she do this to her own boyfriend? Just to make him stay away from me?

I don't know whether I should be fuming with anger because Rashi has gone to such lengths to defame me or sympathise with Sahil for seeing his name splashed on the wall in this demeaning manner. I avoid all the stares and comments of the people around me, and enter the head of the department's cabin teary-eyed.

'May I come in, sir?' I mumble.

'Please.' He looks up from his computer to look at me.

'So, Miss Nandini Kashyap, what is this all about?' He is seeking an answer but I have none. 'We admitted you to the college because your aunt knew one of the faculty members who had told me about your medical condition.'

Oh, so he knows about my memory loss. I think to myself. *But what he doesn't know is that I just learnt that Sahil's surname is Avasthi. And if that's the case, then how could I have been the one to paint it on the wall?*

He continues, 'And now you are being a bully.'

I don't want to cut him off but I have to speak up for myself. 'Sir, I didn't do anything. You need to believe me.'

'Instead of apologising, you are arguing with me. That's not expected for sure.' He says in a straightforward and no-nonsense manner.

'I am sorry, sir,' I apologise.

'Look, I am letting you go with a warning this time. But if I find you misbehaving again, I'll suspend you. This time, I am being courteous and not even informing your aunt because of your health condition. But remember, you're on thin ice.'

'I am really sorry, sir.' I move out of the cabin quietly. I could have blamed Rashi, but there are a couple of reasons behind my silence. One is obvious: I have no proof. Secondly, I don't want us to take this ugly situation back home, especially when the head of the department is ready to let it go this time. The moment

I step out, I run to the main gate to avoid speaking to anyone, not because I feel embarrassed—I hardly care about anyone's opinion at this point—but because I just want some space.

What will Sahil think? He's already so mad at me and after today, he'll treat me like a pariah. Different thoughts haunt me on my way back home. And, of course, I bump into the one person I definitely want to avoid right now.

'What have you done, Nandini?' Sahil asks me.

Speak of the devil.

'Nothing,' I answer. All this while, Sahil has been avoiding me, and now, I want to do the same. I have no courage to face him. So, I start walking away from him, but he follows me. When he doesn't stop following me even after some time, I give up and turn around. He is right behind me. His eyes are blank; I don't know what he is feeling. He takes a step forward and bends down close to me. Our faces are just inches apart.

'Look, Sahil,' I stutter. 'I know you won't believe me. But I didn't do it.'

He looks at me like no one has before and says, 'Really?'

What does he mean by that? Have I convinced him that it wasn't me who did this shameful act? I try to find my answers by looking at the expressions on his face, but his intense look makes it difficult.

'You will stoop down to this level now? Just to defame me,' he says.

No, I didn't. In fact, Rashi wants to defame me. It isn't about you; it is about me. I want to tell him the truth but the words get stuck in my throat.

'Wait, you are wrong.' That's all I manage to say. Before I can say anything more, he cuts me off.

'You are driving me crazy. First you pretend not to know me and now you do this. And then you claim you and I meant nothing to each other.'

He rolls his finger down my cheek. I'm surprised my heart doesn't explode when he does that. I am tempted to touch him back but I resist.

What's wrong with me? Why do I feel such a strong urge to touch him?

He smirks at me when he notices my uneasiness. 'If you want to say such nasty things about me, you should remember that I can do the same.'

I let out a sigh and look down. 'Believe it or not, I am not the one who wrote it.'

The next second, he smiles at me and says, 'I know it wasn't you who did it.'

I am not expecting him to say that. His words have baffled me and I wait for him to explain.

'And now I know that you haven't changed a bit. I can still manipulate you,' he says.

Did he manipulate me in the past too? Does he believe I am innocent?

'What do you mean? You really believe that I didn't do it?' I ask.

'Yes. I was just kidding. I know you cannot do something like this. With whatever time we have spent together in the past, at least I know this cannot have been you.'

My eyes turn moist and I turn and walk away into the crowd, not wanting Sahil to see me emotional. But someone else stops me.

'Nandini, are you alright?' It is Rudra. He must have seen my gloomy face.

I smile at him, until I see Sahil walking towards us behind Rudra. Maybe Rudra is unaware of what has happened.

'I am fine. Thanks.' I can't continue because Sahil has come closer now, and I cannot help but shift my gaze from Rudra to him.

'Last time I asked, you didn't come with me for coffee. You can't refuse today.' Though I am talking to Rudra and can hear what he is saying, my eyes are still fixed on Sahil.

Nervously, I respond, 'You mean now?'

'Yes, why not?' Rudra looks happy, but I am terrified. I can see that Sahil does not like Rudra being friendly with me. After all, his friend is unknowingly trying his luck with his ex-girlfriend.

'No, sorry. I need to rush,' I say. Before he can respond, I run away from both of them.

8

Sahil: The Smoke of Love

Have you ever been betrayed? Do you know what it feels like to be betrayed? Especially by someone you trusted more than yourself? You have pictured your entire life with them, and then one day you wake up and they are gone. I truly believe that relationships should come with a warning: Handle with care!

I had truly loved Nandini. We were made for each other, at least I had thought so. Until that day when I got a message from her. I had told my best friend Kartik about it. I don't know how I would have dealt with the post-breakup trauma without him. He speaks nonsense most of the time but still succeeds in bringing a smile to my face. He is shocked to hear that Nandini is back in my life.

'You mean she is the same girl? Your ex-girlfriend?' he asks sipping vodka from his glass.

'Go slow, brother,' I say, watching him finish the drink in one go. But his attention is focussed on me. He wants to know more.

'*Bhai, meri saari utar gayi yeh sunke*,' he laughs. Kartik makes light of every serious discussion. I can never figure out whether he does this to calm his nerves or if he enjoys such situations.

'Yes, she's the one.' I pour us both another drink. We have been sitting at one of the local bars since evening and I have lost count of how much we have had to drink. 'I never told you this, but after reading her message, I had tried to contact her in every way possible. But I hadn't known any of her immediate family except her mother. And they both had vanished from their house,' I sigh.

The memories come rushing back. I had been heartbroken and shattered after receiving her message, not knowing what to do. Why had she done that to me? 'I had felt lost. I couldn't bear the pain. Her mobile remained not reachable for weeks; she must have changed her number so I wouldn't be able to contact her,' I continue.

'But why is she back now? And that too in Kangra?' Kartik asks. I want to tell him that I am looking for the same answers.

'I seriously don't know. I decided to pursue college in Kangra because every corner of Khajjiar would remind me of her. My parents were more than happy with my decision, since Dad being one of the trustees of our college, had always wanted me to shift here. How could I have known that just when I felt I had moved on, Nandini would break me apart again.'

'Isn't it strange how we allow the same person to break our hearts again and again?' Kartik asks.

I place my hand on his to console him. He, too, is going through bad phase—a breakup. 'I know what you mean. But at least Megha doesn't pretend to not know you,' I say. Kartik and Megha broke up a couple of months ago.

'Yes, she doesn't pretend to not know me but what's the point? She didn't come to college for almost a month after we broke up. No messages, no phone calls. Nothing. And now, she avoids me in college,' Kartik laments.

I can understand that Kartik is hurt, but what Nandini is doing is beyond comprehension. I tell him that. 'Megha just avoids you. She is hurt. But Nandini claims that she has fucking never met me before. That she doesn't know me. What the fuck is that? Is she even serious?'

Kartik takes a deep breath and brings his attention back to Nandini, 'But do you believe she wrote that on the wall today?'

'No, she cannot do it. And why would she write down her own name on the wall if she had actually done it? The professor is a fool, I am not. Anyway, I don't care who did it.'

I know Nandini would never defame me like this. It isn't in her nature. What bothers me though is the realisation that I still love her. For the next couple of hours, Kartik and I continue drinking. When the bar is about to close, I feel a stronge urge to call Nandini. I have somehow found her new number and check her WhatsApp status regularly. But I never text her or call her because I am still annoyed with her. Today, however, I just have to tell her everything that I haven't been able to so far. I have been holding it in my heart for far too long.

'Hello ...' she answers in a shaky voice.

I wonder how it is that the voice that would give me goosebumps a year ago, is still leaving me wanting more. I have been avoiding her in college since day one because the more I see her, the more I want to talk to her, the more likely I was to break the walls that I had built around my heart. I don't respond for a few seconds. Even she doesn't say anything more. I don't know what the time is but the town has gone silent. It seems the darkness in my heart has consumed the entire town too. Apart from a few street lights that are giving hope and direction, there is no one around other than Kartik. But in the silence, I can hear the sound of her breathing and I am sure she can hear mine.

Finally, I hear her voice again. 'Sahil?'

Not a word comes out of my mouth. I should be in awe of how she can still know it's me just by listening to my breath. But the first thought that enters my mind is, *She's lying. She hasn't forgotten anything.*

And just as I feel she is about to hang up, I mumble, 'Nandini.'

The next moment, she replies softly, 'Hey, Sahil.'

Every time she takes my name, my heart skips a beat. I still love her, no matter how much I may deny it. She still has the same effect on me.

'You finally picked up,' I say. 'And even today you can sense it's me.'

She ignores the latter part and replies, 'What do you mean by finally? Did you call earlier too? Did you call on my previous number?'

I am pretty drunk by now and when I hear her say that, I lose control. I scream at her, 'So, you remember you used to have another phone number. But you don't remember that you had a boyfriend. That's funny, right?'

Nandini instantly replies, 'No, it isn't funny ...' She pauses, as if something inside her is stopping her from completing the sentence. I don't know what she was going to say but she changes the topic and blatantly asks, 'What's wrong?'

I laugh; she might have realised I am drunk. 'What's wrong? You should ask what's right as everything you are doing is wrong. Every single thing,' I stress. How can she so shamelessly ask what is wrong?

'Sahil, are you drunk?' she asks.

She can sense it. I ignore her question and continue shouting angrily at her, 'Why did you disappear a year ago with no explanation? I went to your house, I called you so many times, but you just vanished.'

Every word that is coming out of my mouth represents the scars on my heart. The wall that I have built around it is slowly breaking and making me vulnerable again.

She audibly shudders at the bitterness in my tone. I try to picture her expression through her voice as she asks, 'Where are you?'

I ignore her question again and let the wall break further, 'What do you want? I thought I was done with you. Your chapter was over. But you have ruined everything again, Nandini, and I want to know why.'

'Sahil ...' She shrieks out my name but it falls on deaf ears as I continue, 'And then you pretend not to know me. You used to tell me that you won't be able to live without me even for a day. I wonder who the real Nandini is—the one you used to be or the one you are now.' I exhale in disgust, 'You are the most selfish and heartless girl I have ever met. You can't just play with my feelings. I'll not let you to do that.'

'Sahil, where are you?' She speaks so loudly that I immediately stop talking. I take a deep breath and say, 'With Kartik. Near the main market petrol pump.'

'Alright.'

Her 'alright' annoys me even more, 'What's alright? Nothing is right. You don't get it.'

'Wait right there. Sahil, I am coming to meet you. Right now.'

'Why?' It seems more like an order than a question. 'Why do you want to come and meet a stranger?' I pause, 'Oh, you want to see how wasted I am right now? So that you can tell the entire college about it again?'

She sighs in exasperation, 'Just stay there.'

I want to meet her too; I want to hug her and feel her in my arms once more. I have tried to hide my emotions around her from day one but I just cannot anymore. After consuming more than a bottle of vodka, I am trying hard to find composure.

What's happening with me? Why am I still so attracted to her? There are times I want to deny my feelings, but then I get drawn towards her again.

Uncertainty has enveloped me in a swirling fog of mixed emotions. I can't gauge what is right and what isn't anymore. My subconscious mind is asking me if I am doing the right thing. Kartik's statement pops up in my mind again. *Isn't it strange how we allow the same person to break our hearts again and again?*

I reject her overtures against my will, 'No, thanks. I don't need you right now. I don't need you ever.'

But she doesn't budge and says, 'I don't care whether you need me or not. I am coming.'

'Whatever,' I say and disconnect the call.

It's said that every storm subsides with time, but this one seems endless.

9

Nandini: A Night to Forget

No matter how much we plan, it's always the unexpected that ends up shaping our lives. And since it is unexpected, we have no control over it. I didn't say a word to Rashi about what had happened in college after coming home. I felt I owed that to Maasi. I wasn't being submissive, just realistic. Moreover, her intentions don't really matter. I don't want to be around Sahil anyway. Or do I?

Am I really in two minds? Am I once again falling for Sahil? Even though I don't remember falling for him the first time.

Different thoughts haunt me but one thing is certain: I don't want to be the ruthless person that Sahil believes me to be. It is getting on my nerves and just as I am trying to forget about it—at least for today—I get a call from Sahil. I hadn't expected him to call me. At first, I think he has accidently called me or that he wants to blame me once again. I am partially right. But it isn't his fault. My hands start trembling when I hear him breathe on the phone and I know it is him calling me.

But why has he called? Once he starts speaking, I know the call is deliberate. Sahil has so far been rude and emotionless with me in person. But he sounds different on the phone. He is gentle. He sounds genuinely hurt. And the way he bombards me with questions, my heart starts tugging with guilt. I cannot stop myself from wanting to know more about him. About us.

So, I tell him in exasperation, 'Sahil, I am coming to meet you. Right now.'

This conversation can't happen on the phone. Maasi and uncle have gone to a relative's place in Shimla to attend a funeral and will be back only tomorrow. Maasi had wanted me to come along but I assured her countless times that I would be all right. Maasi is also relying on Rashi staying at home with me, but she leaves for a friend's house soon after.

I leave the house hastily without even thinking if I'll get a cab. Luckily, I do, even though it is raining heavily outside. I reach the petrol pump soon. If Maasi ever comes to know that I stepped out of the house at this late hour, she will surely get upset. But I want to do this for myself. I am not going in search of Sahil, I am going in search of myself. While I cannot deny the suffering Sahil has had to go through because of me, it is important we speak to each other. I find Sahil sitting on a roadside bench along with his friend Kartik. Even from a distance, I can make out that he is drunk—much more than I had expected. They are drenched because of the rain, but seem oblivious to that. They keep talking to each other without noticing that I am around.

'So, what are you going to do now?' Kartik asks Sahil. He empties half of the cold drink bottle and mixes vodka in it. 'Now that you have told her what you went through, did it make a difference?' After shaking the bottle well, he hands it over to Sahil, who isn't even able to hold it properly.

'Nothing.'

I watch as Sahil takes a sip directly from the bottle. He isn't able to sit upright or even speak clearly. He is about to say something to Kartik when I go stand in front of him.

'Sahil?'

'Nandini, you are here?' I can see the look of surprise in his eyes. He certainly wasn't expecting me to actually come down to see him.

I try to pull the bottle of vodka away from him, but he resists. I hold him by his arm and help him to stand up. 'Stop acting like a drunkard. I'll drop you guys home.'

'No ...' he shouts. His face is dripping with the drops of rain falling on him. The day seems to have escaped him, disappearing into an alcohol-infused abyss. 'Wait. I don't want to go.'

I look at Kartik and I think he understands what Sahil actually means.

'You guys stay here. Have a word.' He tries to smile, his eyes red because of the alcohol. 'I'll leave.'

'You're sure?' I ask him sincerely. Though he is equally drunk, he seems to be in a better state than Sahil. 'I mean, will you be able to go alone?'

'Yes, I will manage,' he nods.

I hail him a cab and tell him to reach home safely. I focus on Sahil who is unaware of what is happening around him. I had come thinking that I would have a word with him, but he is barely able to move.

'Sahil?

'Hmm?' His eyelids are drooping. He has almost fallen asleep.

'Now, shall we leave? What's your address?' I just want to get him home. But he doesn't answer. He isn't in a state to answer. I sit next to him and Sahil's head falls on my shoulder. The rain has drenched me too by then. It is as if the heavens have decided to unite us again or drown us together in the storm.

A cab stops in front of us and I help him get in, 'We can talk in the cab.'

'I don't want to go home,' he protests.

'Okay, then, we'll going to my home.' I have no option left by then.

I get into the cab and tell the driver my address. Throughout the journey, I keep looking at Sahil. He seems to be an altogether different person. Someone I have neither met nor seen before. I have always thought of him as someone arrogant and insolent because of the way he has been behaving with me. But the Sahil sitting with me in the cab seems hurt, shattered and heartbroken. When we reach Maasi's place, the driver has to help me pull Sahil out of the cab and take him inside the house.

Once inside, he tries to balance himself on his own feet. Somehow, he manages to turn his head towards me, still using my shoulders as support and murmurs, 'Nandini?'

'Yeah. I am right here,' I reply as I take him to my room.

'Why, Nandini, why?' He keeps repeating.

I feel terribly guilty. But I calmly reply, 'We will talk tomorrow. Now is not the right time.'

I think he understands me because he hits the bed and seems to pass out. But after a few minutes of silence where I just observe him, Sahil opens his eyes and continues with his questions.

'This is ridiculous. You say the same thing every time. You ghosted me. Did you even love me?' He says all this in one breath. His frustration is obvious.

I wish I remembered why I had decided to leave him. Clearly, it haunts both of us.

I feel bad for him and even though I know he cannot hear me, I say softly, 'I am sorry, Sahil.'

But he grabs hold of my hand as if he has heard me and says, 'Was I not good enough for you?'

Before I can say anything, he falls back into deep sleep. I watch him and think to myself, *I don't know what to say. Is this the real you or are you the person you portray to be every day in college? I wish I could do something to help you; I wish I had the answers to your questions. But I am helpless and it disgusts me. Sometimes I feel I should tell you about my memory loss. But how would it make any difference? It won't change anything. I will still not remember you. I don't even know how you will react when you wake up here tomorrow. I wish I could understand you. But you remain one of the many unsolved puzzles of my life.*

I don't realise when I doze off too. The next morning when my eyes open, I see that Sahil has just woken up as well. It is still dark outside. My eyes immediately go to where the box containing my old phone is kept. If Sahil checks it, he will find our pictures together. That would only make the situation worse. Fortunately, the box is untouched. When he sees me, he instantly asks, 'What are you up to?' His eyes are still red. I can tell he is badly hungover by the way he is holding his head.

'Sorry?' I look at him and get up from my bed. I realise that I had fallen asleep in my wet clothes. But they are almost dry by now. 'Don't you think you are being rude again?'

He gives me his typical sarcastic laugh, 'And don't you think it's rude to pretend not to recognise someone you once knew so closely? You also keep lying shamelessly. The story you tell about your parents; that's complete bullshit. Your mom raised you singlehandedly.'

I am too stunned to say anything and take a deep breath. I wasn't aware of any of this. Maasi has never mentioned anything about my parents, and I have always assumed that they both died in the same car crash which had put me in a coma. But it seems that isn't the case. I try again to recollect my past, but there is nothing.

I ignore his taunt as well as the information he has revealed inadvertently, and remind him, 'You called me last night, if you remember.'

'Wow,' he exclaims. I don't think he expected me to say that. 'I am sorry. I was drunk. I won't ever do that again.'

There he goes again! Mr Sahil Avasthi. And now I am not sure whether he is just pretending like nothing happened or he genuinely doesn't remember anything.

I break the silence after what seems like a long pause and say, 'Yes, I am sure you won't. So, what now?'

'Listen, Nandini.' He walks towards me and grabs me tightly by my shoulders. This hurts me and he can clearly sense that, but he doesn't let go of me, 'All these days you have been pretending not to know me and then you bring me to your house? I really don't know what you are up to. But if you think we can get back together, you are mistaken. I'll never forgive you.'

He pushes me away and opens the bedroom door with full force. As he steps out, I hear the sound of the main door opening. I rush outside to see who it could be.

Rashi! What the fuck! I wasn't expecting her to come home so soon. Especially after a night out.

As I stand there, I wish I had a magical wand to make myself disappear. But this is my life now and I know I have messed up.

'What are you doing here?' Sahil asks Rashi. He seems as shocked to see her as I am.

Rashi's eyes had widened on seeing Sahil. But hearing his question, she regains her composure. 'This is my house. And I should be the one asking this question.' She looks at me angrily and continues, 'Last night, you said you were busy. This was your work? Sleeping with my sister?' She shifts her gaze to Sahil, expecting a response.

A few hours ago, she had tried to defame me in college and had warned me to stay away from Sahil. And now she had seen us stepping out of my bedroom together. I am terrified to think of what she will do next.

'She's your sister?' he asks, looking at me. I am silent and can hardly look into his eyes.

'Unfortunately, yes,' Rashi instantly replies, 'But that doesn't answer my question. What were the two of you doing together all night?'

I had been planning to tell Sahil to leave, when Rashi had returned the house. Maasi wasn't going to be back before the evening and it had been a safe bet to think that no one would get to know that I had got a boy home with me. But that was not to be. And, even though nothing had happened, it was going to be difficult to prove that we hadn't done anything.

'Whatever. It has nothing to do with you,' Sahil replies. Without another word to either of us, he leaves the house.

An air of melancholy strangles me and all I feel is numbness.

10

Nandini: I Miss My Parents

'Mom, she has crossed all limits today. You can't keep supporting her now,' Rashi is yelling at the top of her voice. Just like I had expected, she had revealed everything to Maasi and uncle as soon as they had entered the house. That has resulted in a round table conference which I am forced to attend as well. 'I had told you to look for a youth care centre for her and keep her out of our house. You didn't listen to me. Now see what she has done.'

Maasi doesn't say a word. She is understandably upset but she doesn't know the whole truth. She asks me about what actually happened and when I tell her, she realises that I have done nothing wrong. But Rashi doesn't stop with her tantrums.

'She's lying. It's in her genes. Why don't you understand?'

What the fuck does she mean by that? And how can she speak about me and my parents in that way! Though I don't have any memories of my parents, she has no right to say such nasty things about my genes. 'Rashi, stay within your limits. I haven't said a word yet, but that doesn't mean I am scared of you. You better mind your words,' I say.

'I am not talking to you, bitch. Keep your mouth shut!' she shrieks again.

In an instant, Maasi gets up from her chair and raises her hand to slap Rashi, but uncle stops her. I don't understand why he does that because she does deserve a slap. Maasi is livid. 'Rashi, will you please calm down, so that we can sort this out. I have talked to Nandini and it's not what you think it is,' Maasi says and settles back in her chair and starts taking long, deep breaths.

That worries me because I don't want her blood pressure to shoot up because of Rashi and me. But Rashi doesn't give up and continues, 'Stop acting so innocent, Mom. You remember what happened in the past, right?' Rashi pauses after saying this. Maasi's face turns pale on hearing Rashi's words. She gestures for Rashi to stop talking, but Rashi is beyond listening. 'You are repeating the same mistake again,' she says.

I am shaken by what I have heard. What has Maasi been hiding? Which mistake is Rashi referring to? Is that the reason why Maasi always chickens out from telling me anything when I ask her about my past?

'Today, one guy has come home, tomorrow there'll be another one.' Rashi gets up from her seat to show her authority. By this time, even Uncle's face has fallen. 'I don't mind whatever she does out of this house, but tell her to stay away from my friends,' she screams.

Maasi knows Rashi has crossed all limits of decency this time. She gets up and slaps Rashi hard. Rashi has started getting on my nerves too, so I don't hold back either. 'You mean your boyfriend?' I want her secrets to be out too in front of her parents.

'Yes, my boyfriend. So what?' Despite getting slapped by her mother, Rashi goes on shouting shamelessly. She picks up a glass from the table and throws it on the floor in anger. 'Your mother used to do the same thing and now you are following in her footsteps.'

That is it. I have had enough. I hold her arm and twist it behind her back as hard as I can. She starts shouting in pain but I don't care. 'Look, say whatever you want to about me ... like you always do. But don't fucking bring my mom in between. I am warning you. I won't keep quiet just because this family has done me favours. I won't listen to a single word against my parents,' I say.

I don't know what has got into me but I am reacting in the way my heart is telling me to. Uncle finally steps in between us after hearing my last sentence. He has been quiet all this while, but not anymore. 'Will you girls just stop all this? For God's sake! What have you both turned into? And, Rashi, you ...' He looks at her furiously, 'Have you stopped respecting your mother, too, in your rage?'

No one says anything for a while. All of a sudden, it feels as if the storm has subsided. The room turns hauntingly silent. No one meets anyone else's eyes.

Rashi breaks the silence, 'Yes, you are right. What have I turned into?' she sighs. Tears are rolling down her cheeks as she says this. 'You should ask yourself, Dad, about why I have become like this.' I can't comprehend her words but then she turns towards me and says, 'What I said is the truth, no matter how harsh it may seem to you. Your mother was sleeping with my father and if you don't believe me, ask my mother.'

I don't know how true her words are. But at this moment I feel as if it would have been better if I had never woken up from my coma. Rashi points towards Maasi. 'She saw them together just like I saw you today. Oh no, I was a little late, your bedroom act was over by then. But she was right on time. Now, like your mother, you too are trying to snatch away someone who is not yours.'

I was wrong. The storm hasn't subsided. Rather, it had just been the lull before the storm—a storm that is threatening to knock me to the ground, leaving me breathless, alone and weak. Rashi hadn't been lying. Maasi's silence and the expressions on uncle's face are speaking clearly. I feel like screaming because I seem to have lost whatever little hope, control and power I thought I had. I am heartbroken and my feet are refusing to move, knowing that no one and nothing can save me from this storm. Not even myself. How I wish I never knew the truth.

I am sitting alone in my room unable to stop myself from crying. I cannot process what just happened. Was this trauma worse than the one I had gone through after the accident? Maybe. Maybe not. But I had been unconscious at that time and hadn't really felt the pain. But this pain now is just unbearable. What is the truth about my parents? What don't I know? Sahil had said earlier that my mom had raised me singlehandedly. Is this the reason Dad had left us? I have several questions, but no answers.

I turn my phone on to divert my mind just as Uncle knocks on my door. He sees the tears rolling down my cheeks and fakes a smile to make me feel better. But I am disgusted to see him. I cannot imagine him being with my mother. He sits on the bed near me, taking the support of his hand to settle his body. He looks at me thoughtfully and says, 'You know what, Nandini, life cannot be always seen in white and black. Most of the time it's full of shades of grey.' His eyes look like he has been hiding something for a long time. I turn towards him, wiping my tears as he continues, 'We all shared a very good bond with your mother as she often came to Kangra for work and also because she used to visit the Bajreshwari temple.'

'Bajreshwari temple?' I ask.

'Yes. She was a part of the main religious group of the temple and had tremendous faith in the goddess.'

I shouldn't be sitting with the man who allegedly had an affair with my mother, but I cannot stop myself. Because for the first time someone is actually talking to me about my mother and her life. I keep listening to whatever he is saying. 'We would often go on outings together. She loved you a lot and she did everything possible to make you happy. Regardless of her struggles, she always had a smile on her face,' he says. A smile appears on his face thinking about my mother.

I gain some courage and ask, 'What about your relation—' I can't complete the sentence but we both know what I am talking about. I want to know the truth.

'What Rashi said ... that's not true,' he quickly responds, rubbing his eyes. He is breathing heavily, trying to make sure he doesn't break down in front of me. After a brief pause, he looks into my eyes, and says, 'It was just a weak moment. But before we could cross our limits, your mother realised it was wrong. I agreed with her. Nothing really happened. But I carry the burden of that day even today.'

He gets up from the bed and walks towards the window. 'However, that day everything changed. Everyone blamed us. Despite not doing anything, we were labelled cheaters. She never visited this house after that. It was all because of one misunderstanding.'

He is staring out of the window, lost in his thoughts. Maybe he has never shared this with anyone before. Or maybe no one believes him. Either way, I have no words for him. It is too much information to process in a day. He turns towards me, his hands tucked inside his pockets and says, 'You need to know one thing, Nandini ...' He pauses and I look up at him, my eyes still moist, '... Your mother was a strong woman.'

11

Megha: He Crushed My Heart

I place my order at the counter and go back to the table Nandini is occupying.

'Here's your thupka.' I move the bowl towards her once the order arrives, 'Have it. It looks yummy.'

Nandini is lost in her own thoughts and doesn't hear me. I snap my fingers in front of her face. 'Are you alright?' I ask.

'Yes,' she says in a muffled voice. She sounds low and is clearly not alright. I know she is thinking about what had happened in college a few days ago—the incident with the paint on the wall. We hadn't met since then. I had called her and called her, but she hadn't answered any of my calls. I had even waited for her at the college gate to go to the café with her, but she never turned up. That was two days ago. She has been ignoring me since then. And now here she is , sitting in front of me and still thinking about the same incident.

'I was really worried about you. I called you so many times. You left that day without informing me.'

She looks up at me to say, 'Sorry for backing out of our café plan without telling you.'

I gasp on hearing that. 'Oh! Come on! You think I was calling you about our outing?' Nandini maintains a poker face, but I can sense her pain. I hold her hand to comfort her. 'I was worried about you. I care about you a lot.'

She frowns and asks, 'You think I did it?' She is referring to the words sprayed on the wall.

I frown harder. 'Of course not, Nandini.' I brush aside her question and ask, 'But who would do that and why?'

'Rashi.'

I choke on my thupka and wipe my mouth with a tissue before saying, 'Rashi? Why would she do something like this? What a bitch!'

'It's complicated,' Nandini responds, sipping on the coke that had come along with the thupka.

I am not convinced and have no intention of letting it go so easily. I probe further, 'There must be something behind all this. It must be related to Sahil.' I pause to see if she reacts. I hit the right spot. Her eyes widen immediately. 'I mean, I have seen you guys sharing occasional glances. Is something cooking between you guys?' I pause again to study her expressions. Something *is* definitely wrong. 'And Rashi is jealous?' I ask.

'Stop making up stories,' Nandini exclaims.

I still insist. 'There has to be a reason …'

'It's because …' Nandini starts, a stormy note in her voice. 'Rashi is my cousin and she feels I am coming between her and Sahil.'

'What do you mean by *between?*' I ask, 'As far as I know they aren't in a relationship.'

'What?' Nandini is shocked to hear me say that.

'Yes,' I reply as if my answer is obvious. But why is she looking so surprised?

'How do you know?' she asks.

'Through a common friend,' I sigh, lowering my eyes and continue, 'It's got something to do with that long story that I had referred to on the day we met for the first time.'

'Tell me.' Nandini leans forward and folds her hands in anticipation.

'Why do you want to know?' I wink and she stares back at me. 'I mean, why are you so keen to know about Sahil's relationship status? Surely something is cooking right?'

'It's complicated,' she repeats.

'This is also complicated? Is something going on or do you have a past with him? What is it?'

Nandini seems caught in a fix. 'Nothing. I just want to know why Rashi dragged my name into this whole mess,' she says. But her answer doesn't convince me.

Before I can ask her anything more, she says, 'You were telling me about your story. What about it?'

'Now that's definitely not complicated.' I bite my bottom lip nervously. I look around to make sure nobody can overhear us before saying, 'Promise me you won't tell anyone.'

When she nods, I continue. 'I was in a relationship with Kartik, Sahil's best friend. We got together at the beginning of our first year of college.'

'Oh really, how did you guys meet?' The smile that has been missing from her face since the first day we met, now flashes brightly.

I let my mind drift back to the moment when I had met Kartik for the first time. 'It was in the canteen during our first week of college. We met while placing orders for our food and just started talking. Soon we were interacting daily and before I knew it, we had started dating. It was casual between us, but it was certainly very special for me. Because every time I was with him, I would feel an adrenaline rush, a rush I had never experienced with anyone before.'

Every memory with him is still fresh in my mind. He had been wearing a grey shirt the day he told me he loved me. I still remember the location, the date and every minute detail of that conversation. My smile turns wistful and bitter, as I suddenly remember how we had parted ways. 'But it lasted only for a year because he broke my heart.'

'What? How?' Nandini is taken aback. The smile on her face has disappeared again.

'I hadn't expected him to behave the way did.' I was getting agitated and my nostrils were flaring. 'He made me feel inferior because of my disability.'

Nandini watches my face fall as tears prick my eyes. Just the mention of Kartik's name upsets me. Moreover, seeing him every day in college makes the situation even worse. I had avoided going to college initially, but how long could I have continued with that? I had to face reality. And I was still trying to move on from him.

Nandini reaches for my hand and gives it a comforting squeeze, 'Do you regret the relationship?'

I shrug, 'He shouldn't have done that.' I am still heartbroken and that reflects in my voice.

Kartik has broken my heart into many small pieces, but I am not ready to put it back together. If there's anything worse than a broken heart, it is that you never saw it coming.

Nandini looks into my eyes with sympathy. She must be feeling the pain I have been hiding for so long. But her next words surprise me. 'You should give him a chance to explain.'

'It's easy for you to say that. This idea that love should be about forgiving, that's all bullshit.' I punch the table with my hand in anger and continue, 'But only someone who has been hurt and betrayed knows how it feels. What would you do if you were in my shoes?'

I don't wait for her answer and get lost in my thoughts.

I had believed Kartik would never hurt me because he always made feel loved. Now I am beginning to question my sanity. My world has fallen apart and I am utterly distraught. Kartik had been my world, and he had betrayed me and hurt me to a degree beyond my comprehension. He had lied to me, manipulated my words and faked his love. If destiny hadn't wanted us to be together, then why had we crossed paths with each other in the first place? Why am I unable to get over him? Sometimes it feels like the universe is conspiring against me. Why did we have to meet, only for me to be shattered into pieces?

For a moment, I get carried away with my feelings. But I realise it is better to shrug them off. When the wounds are fresh, they hurt more if you think about them. Nandini sees my discomfort and brings the conversation back to where it had started from.

'So, Kartik told you that Sahil isn't in a relationship with Rashi?'

'How insensitive is that!' I grin, sensing that Nandini is still wondering how I know Sahil isn't in a relationship. 'I narrate my break-up story to you and you show no sympathy. All you are interested in is whether Sahil is single. And then you tell me you feel nothing for him,' I say, my voice full of mischief. We both burst out laughing.

12

Nandini: I Need You

Another doomed relationship, another pair of broken hearts! Life isn't as simple as it seems. It keeps pushing us down, challenging us again and again to get up. But I have realised by now that it is these challenges that keep you alive. There are lessons to be learnt at every step of life.

'It's easy for you to say that. This idea that love should be about forgiving, that's all bullshit.'

Megha's words had pierced my heart. She had asked me what I would have done if I'd been in her shoes. But what she hadn't known was that Kartik's shoes were better suited for me. However, had I really cheated on Sahil? The incidents of the past few days had weighed me down and pushed me into an abyss. When my uncle had told me that my mother had been a strong woman, I had felt touched. But I know it must have been true. I just needed to trust my instincts. Just like I trusted my instincts about Rudra even though Megha had warned me about him when we were in the canteen.

'I see that Rudra is trying hard to impress you. But don't be fooled by his looks,' Megha had said. 'It's better to maintain a safe distance from him.'

'But why?' I had asked her, confused.

'Because he's not someone you can trust. He often plays with the feelings of girls. For him, a one-night stand is no big deal.'

'But he has always been nice to me.'

I had tried to defend him, not because I felt anything romantic towards him, but because by then I had already agreed to go out for a coffee with him. I had got out of it a couple of times by making some excuse or the other. But if anyone had been paying attention, they would have known that I was lying both times. In spite of that, each time Rudra had said, 'No worries, another time?' and I had replied, 'Of course'. I knew I couldn't put him off forever. If I didn't plan on going out with him, I should have just told him that straight away so that he could have moved on. I hadn't done that.

But if what Megha had said is true and going out with him is a bad idea, I don't think I want to meet him now. Moreover, I am still upset about the chaos at home.

Even now, though a couple of days have passed after that huge scene at home, I am still not totally over it. Maasi can sense it because for the last forty-eight hours we have hardly interacted with each other which is rare. Different thoughts keep plaguing me since that big revelation and I still don't know whom to trust.

If so much had happened in the past, why has Maasi always been so nice to me? Should I trust what Rashi had said or what my uncle had confessed? If what Rashi had said was true, I don't know how to continue facing my Maasi, as it is because of my mother that her family life has been disrupted, the wounds of which still seem to be fresh in everyone's minds. Had my father left my mother because of this incident? And after all that has happened in the last couple of days, will my relationship with Maasi ever be the same again?

I have no answers to all these questions that make me restless. But in the evening, Maasi approaches me and tries to break the awkwardness that has crept up between us. She takes me on a ride with her, probably expecting that I would have a lot of questions for her. As expected, I do.

'Maasi, I want to ask you something,' I say as I look at her as she drives the car.

'Sure.' She turns her head towards me and smiles. Her expressions reveal that she already knows what is coming her way.

We have been living together for weeks now, but in the past I have never persisted with my questions whenever she has refused to answer me. It isn't that I hadn't wanted to know; I have always had a feeling that she is hiding something from me because she doesn't want to hurt me. And that turned out to be true. But was that all there was to the story or was there more? Today I want all the answers.

'Did my dad leave us because he also believed what you had seen between my mother and my uncle?'

'No, not at all,' she replies. 'Your father was a coward. He abandoned you even before your birth. It had nothing to do with this incident. He broke all of his marriage commitments a long time ago and left your mother alone during her pregnancy.'

Sahil had been right. My mom had raised me singlehandedly. Maasi continues, 'However, your mother did decide to raise you all alone and give you a good life. She never remarried and would do everything only for you.'

When I had seen my mother's photograph in the box all those days ago, I had felt nothing towards her. No emotion. But as I am getting to know her better, I can see how much she must have sacrificed for me. I feel closer to her now. I also feel an urge to find out where my dad is.

'Why did my father decide to leave us?' I ask my Maasi.

'How does that even matter after all these years? It's better we don't talk about him.' Maasi shuts down my train of thought. Her words don't suppress my urge to know more about him. But for now, I decide to let things be.

'You were very close to my mom, right?' I ask looking at her curiously. 'Uncle told me.'

'Very close.' There is laughter in her eyes. A sense of joy as she seems to recollect their time together. 'Since our childhood, we shared everything with each other. I miss her so much.' She sighs and her face looks sad as she says, 'My only regret is that I kept my distance from her after that incident with your uncle. But I truly loved her.' She pauses for a moment. In that silence, I think about how a misunderstanding can turn our lives upside down. She continues, 'I remember she had visited Kangra that month of the accident and had asked me to meet her at the Bajreshwari temple. She had wanted things to go back to normal.'

I can see the regret on Maasi's face. I'm surprised that she is suddenly being so open with me about my mother. She has always said that she would tell me everything when the time was right. I hadn't known what she had meant then, and even now I have no real clue, until she mentions, 'If I hadn't stayed away from her, I would have known what she had been going through in her last days and why she had wanted to shift from Khajjiar.'

'Shift from Khajjiar? Why?' *Had we been leaving the city when we'd had the accident?*

'Yes, that's what she told me when she had called few days before the accident. Though, she hadn't given any reason for the move. Maybe she would have told me, had we still shared the same bond we used to.'

Listening to Maasi, I realise that sometimes things really are beyond our control. If only we could know how things were going to turn out in the future. I take a deep breath and look outside at the cars passing by. 'Will you ever allow me to go to our old home? Maybe it will ring a bell and my memory will return,' I ask her anxiously, not knowing how she will respond.

'Of course,' she says and caresses my hair affectionately. 'When you were in the hospital, I retrieved whatever I could from your old house and eventually sold it. More than half of that money went towards your medical expenses and the rest I have kept for your education and wedding.'

In that moment I realise I don't know what I would have done if Maasi had not been there for me after my accident. That's all I can think about right now and I am so grateful for her presence in my life.

The next day, once our college lectures are over, I walk towards the main gate where Rudra and I have decided to meet. I see him leaning against his car, his arms and legs casually crossed. He is looking at me and smiling. I smile back at him. But it doesn't last long because I spot Sahil and Kartik standing just a few meters away. Whenever I see Sahil, I feel a familiar tug towards him and with each passing day, I trust him more and more. He hadn't been wrong when he'd had claimed that he had been my boyfriend or he had revealed that I had been raised by my mother alone. Also, our encounter on that rainy day when he had rested his head on my shoulders and held me tightly under the rain, has made my heart grow fonder of him. But is it guilt pulling me closer to him or do I have genuine affection for him? The last time we had spoken, he had clearly told me that if I was expecting us to be together again, I was mistaken.

When I greet Rudra, I see Sahil's face change. He stares at me for a couple of seconds and then ignores me, leaving me feeling empty inside. I trudge over to the passenger side of Rudra's car and settle myself in the seat next to him.

'So finally, you decided spending time with me is worth it,' Rudra teases me.

'It's not that,' I say, trying to come up with another excuse. 'It's not easy to adjust to a new place so quickly. I hope you understand.'

'Yes, of course I do. It must be tough to live apart from your parents.'

I stay silent. It is better this way because I don't want him asking me any more questions.

'Where are we heading?' I ask.

'It's a surprise.' His face breaks into a huge smile.

Soon, he is driving through the entrance of a huge five-star hotel. I wish he had forewarned me. I don't fit in places like these. Towering glass doors serve as the entrance, leading to a marbled lobby. I look around and feel underdressed, even though I am wearing an outfit I love.

'I'm not sure I'm classy enough for this place,' I whisper to Rudra as we are being escorted to our table.

'Oh, come on, you are. In fact, you are a queen. Don't underestimate yourself.' Rudra winks at me and I force a smile in return, appreciating his attempt to calm my nerves with humour.

As we take our seats, he continues praising me, 'You look great. That dress really suits you.'

The next half an hour is surreal. The menu has words in a language I don't understand so I resort to safety and say, 'I'll have the same, please' after Rudra places his order. We indulge in light banter as we wait for our meal. He tells me about his college experiences and how he wants to become a content writer.

'What do you want to write about?' I ask him.

He shakes his head, 'Whatever gives me good money.'

'But what do you actually want to write about? What excites you?' I watch as he butters his roll. He looks so natural in this posh setting.

'I think I love writing about people. There are so many real-life stories that are inspiring. I want to pen down those stories and add a touch of entertainment to them.'

'Wow, that sounds interesting,' I reply. By now, I have started to relax. I'm not sure if it is because of the food, the ambience or the company but I am glad I didn't back out of this date.

The biryani that comes soon after to our table is one of the best things I have ever tasted. I had forgotten how good food can make you feel and though I am full I want to eat more. I find that in spite of my initial reluctance and the fear that Megha's warnings had created, I feel refreshed in Rudra's company.

After we finish our meal, Rudra pays the bill and we walk out. I check my Google Maps app and home is less than a thirty-minute cab ride away.

'Why do you want to take a cab? I'll drive you home,' he insists when he sees me booking one.

'No, Maasi won't like it.' I don't want to trouble him and politely decline his offer. I am also looking forward to calling Megha on the way home to tell her how her perception of Rudra had been completely wrong.

He turns to face me and I realise how close he is standing to me. 'Are you sure?' he asks, as his arm brushes against mine.

'Yes, trust me, I'm good.' I nod and thank him, 'I had a great time, Rudra.'

He has behaved like a gentleman throughout our time together. Now he gestures for me to leave first but I tell him to go ahead. Shooting me one last smile, he gets into his car and leaves. I feel like getting some fresh air, so I decide to walk home instead. With every step, I ponder over my life—the same questions, the same mysteries bother me more and more with every passing day. My mother who had treated me like a princess, my father who had shied away from his responsibility even before I was born, my Maasi and uncle whose relationship had become bitter because of a slight transgression, Rashi who is becoming more heartless each day, and Sahil whose memories I don't have but with whom I feel a strong connection.

Lost in my thoughts, I don't realise when Google Maps diverts me onto a narrow back street away from the main road. It is only then that I sense that someone is following me. I walk a few metres, trying to ignore the uncomfortable feeling, but it gets creepier by the minute. There is hardly anyone on the road as it has started raining by now. I turn back to see if by chance I am mistaken. Unfortunately, I am not. A man *is* following me, but I can't see him clearly because of the heavy downpour. Although I have an umbrella to use as a makeshift weapon if the need arises, I am regretting my decision of not going along with Rudra. When the man sees me glancing back, he pretends to look elsewhere. It doesn't take me long to panic and I immediately enter a grocery store to hide. Luckily, the man doesn't enter after me. But I can see him standing outside, hiding under his umbrella. I can't see his face but I am certain he is waiting for me to exit.

Why the fuck is he stalking me? I need to do something, I think to myself.

I scroll through the call history on my phone and dial Maasi's number. But she doesn't pick up. I even call Uncle but even his number is unavailable. I don't know why but instead of calling Rudra, I think of calling Sahil. I had never thought there would come a time when I would need to call him. While I debate on what I should do, I am losing precious time. How long can I stay inside the store? I call Sahil instantly. With every ring, I feel my legs shaking.

He eventually picks up and I breath a sigh of relief. 'Sahil ... please listen ...'

He either ignores my panicked voice or pretends not to notice. 'What do you want?'

Without wasting any more time in wondering why Sahil hadn't sensed my panic, I tell him, 'I need your help, right now.'

'Why do you need me now?' His tone doesn't change. 'Isn't Rudra with you?'

I explain everything and wait for him to respond. But all I get in return is his usual silence.

'Are you there?' I ask.

'Yes.' His voice is softer this time, 'Where are you?'

I tell him I will send him my location and also give him directions. 'Are you coming? Please?'

'But why didn't you call Rudra?'

His continuous probing is pissing me off but I decide to say, 'Because I thought of calling you.'

'Sorry, but I can't come. When I needed you, you weren't there.'

When I hear this, I am engulfed by immense guilt and sadness. Before I can say anything more, Sahil disconnects the call.

13

Sahil: Nandini Kashyap Is Dead

Sometimes the person you'd take a bullet for ends up being the person holding the gun to your head. That's the worst feeling in the world. You have been lied to by someone you trusted. I had felt the same way when Nandini had vanished from my life. I have told her clearly that we can never be together again. Despite not wanting to be with her, I am hurt when I see her walking away with Rudra. I shouldn't feel that way but getting over our relationship had been a difficult process. I hadn't known Rashi was Nandini's sister and since that day, I haven't been receptive to Rashi's advances even though I am aware that she likes me. It would be so easy to try to get back at Nandini by dating Rashi, but that's not me. I don't know how she dumped me so easily, and now pretends to not know me and hangs out with someone else in front of me.

When Nandini called me for help, I had felt exasperated. I hadn't wanted to hear even one word from her. But now after she has finished narrating what is happening with her and on hearing the terror in her voice, I am feeling concerned. Even though I tell her to stop bothering me, as soon as I keep the phone down, I know I will never leave her alone in her predicament. What if she is telling the truth. I immediately leave for the location that she has sent me. It isn't far but it takes me around twenty minutes to reach her. She is still inside the grocery store like she had told me, but when I bring her out of the store, there is no one outside.

'He was right there …' She points towards the other side of the road, '…hiding behind an umbrella. He had been following me for a while.'

'There's no one around, Nandini. See for yourself,' I state, unable to ascertain if she had been telling me the truth on the phone.

We stare at each other for a few seconds when she breaks the silence. 'You said you wouldn't come.'

'Stop it.' I turn away from her and look the other way. There is still no one around. I am furious with myself for having thought that she could have been telling the truth about being in trouble. 'You played me again, Nandini.'

She looks nervous; maybe she is confused by my behaviour. On the one hand, by reaching out to help her, I have practically confessed that I care for her. On the other, the way I speak to her probably makes me seem heartless.

'Do you hate me so much that you are ready to believe that I was lying?' she asks.

'What else am I supposed to do?' I try my best to hide my feelings for her when I say that.

'Okay, thanks for coming. And I am sorry for troubling you.'

What the fuck is she up to? The more I try to comprehend her, the more convoluted it all gets. She turns to walk away. But before she can, I grab her hand and pull her towards me. I want to shout at her and ask why she is doing all this. But when I see her trembling in fear, I say, 'Come along with me. I'll drop you home. Or someone else will start following you.'

'There is no need. I can go alone. And I won't trouble you again.' She tries to release her hand from my grip, but I am too strong for her.

'I don't want to witness any more of your tantrums,' I say and ask her to get in the car.

After ensuring that she is settled in the passenger seat, I go around and get in the car. I stare at her for a moment too long, trying to figure out what she could be hiding. She eventually asks, 'What happened?'

'Nothing.' I ignore my thoughts and start the car. But as I drive, I can't hold back and ask her the same question again, 'Why are you back?'

All I get in return is more silence. Finally, she says, 'You won't believe me …' She turns her gaze away from me and starts looking straight ahead at the road, '… but I am sorry for hurting you in the past.'

I wish I had the strength to stop the car and ask her to get off right away. I wish I could kill the emotions inside me and tell her that I hate her for what she is doing to me. Is she really sorry for having hurt me?

I laugh sarcastically and say, 'You should get an Oscar for your acting. I am totally baffled.'

'I am not acting. I am really sorry for hurting you.' She turns back towards me and sits sideways so she can look me straight in my eyes.

The agony in her words is apparent. It tears at my heart and I struggle to get words out. But I still want answers so I say, 'You still aren't giving me the right answers. Why are you back in my life?'

'I don't have any answers because I myself don't know why I'm back,' she says, her face wrought with misery.

I have had enough of her vague answers. 'What do you mean by you don't know?' I stop the car on the side of the road. I want to tell her how her behaviour has been rattling my brain, 'Since that first day in college, I can see you aren't behaving like you used to. You aren't yourself. You look exactly like the girl I used to know, but somehow you aren't. You are supposed to be in my year, but now you are my junior. You even lied about your parents. Why? Have you lost your mind?'

'You can say that. Yes. I have lost my mind. I didn't know how to tell you.' She stretches her hand to hold mine, and I am taken aback by that. But I don't react to her torn expression. She intertwines her fingers with mine and closes her eyes. I am breathing heavily now. Her touch feels the same; it still mesmerises me. While her eyes are closed, I want to kiss her and forget everything that has happened in the past. In the next moment, she opens her eyes. Hoping that she would give me some answers, I tighten my grip on her hand. But she releases it and says, 'I gave it another try. But I still can't recollect our memories together.'

What the hell! What's wrong with this girl? 'Nandini, enough is enough,' I shout.

She takes a deep breath and starts speaking, 'Will you believe me if I say that I had a car accident a year ago? That I ended up in a coma and lost my memory? That my mother passed away in that accident?'

My face is becoming paler with each sentence from her. My heart beat quickens, but at the same time a feeling of numbness takes over my body. I can feel the walls around me come crashing down as if a wrecking ball has been at work on it. She continues, 'It's not that I am keeping secrets or deliberately being horrid to you. But I seriously don't remember anything from the past.'

I laugh painfully at that, but she continues speaking, as if a dam has broken. 'I can't remember my home. I can't remember my fucking identity. You say that I am lying about my parents, but I don't have even a single memory of my mother. Yes, I lie to people because I don't want to reveal to everyone that I am mentally vulnerable. What more should I tell you? You hate me so much, you probably don't believe anything I am saying, right?' she cries.

It seems like a storm has broken around us, where everything had been calm just moments ago. 'I feel lost. I wish I had died with my mother. She's no more; she's dead. But even after surviving, I feel dead.'

I am shocked by her revelations, but her final words leave me stunned. She lifts her head and finally says, 'Your Nandini Kashyap is dead.'

14

Nandini: Will You Accept Me?

As I let go of all the 'would'ves', 'should'ves' and 'could'ves' that have been weighing me down for so long, I can feel my heart smiling because of how relieved I am. However, sometimes even after a huge burden has been lifted, the relief that one feels doesn't come all at once. That's why I still feel guilty about whatever Sahil has had to go through because of me. Even though he had been repeatedly asking me why I was back, I hadn't been sure of revealing the truth to him. But after he unexpectedly came to save me today, I realised that he still cared for me and that if there was anyone I could trust, it was him. He had come after just one desperate call from me, making me realise that he deserved to know the truth about me even if he didn't believe me.

When I finally reveal the truth, his face remains emotionless. I give him a few minutes to grasp what I have told him. But the longer he stays silent, the more I worry about his eventual outburst. Sahil looks confused as if the information still hasn't sunk in.

After patiently waiting for some more time, he asks in a muffled voice, 'So, you remember nothing?'

I shake my head and say, 'No, I'm sorry.'

'You are lying.' His statement holds a hint of suspicion.

I am taken aback but now that I have confessed it all, I am determined to see it to the end. 'No, I am not. I have avoided you since day one because I have no answers to your questions. I don't have any today either but I feel it is time I revealed the truth to you. I feel I shouldn't hide it anymore. I am not lying. Only I know the pain I am going through. It's not only you who has suffered this past year.'

He is keenly observing me to check if I am actually telling the truth. I know in my heart that he believes me but he probably isn't going to easily forget the horrendous time he has had to go through because of me.

'So why did you tell me today?' he asks.

I sigh, and reveal that it was because what I had seen in his eyes. 'Because you still care about me.'

He certainly isn't expecting that answer to his question. His grip on the steering tightens as if there is a volcano of emotions bubbling inside him that might erupt any minute. Without looking into my eyes, he asks, 'What all did you forget?'

'Everything,' I answer.

He falls into a silence and stays deep in thought for some time, before his eyes turn back towards me. I don't know what he had been thinking about, but the look in his eyes is different. Something I have never seen before. There is a certain tenderness on his face. I wonder if that is merely out of sympathy or if his feelings for me have undergone a change after my revelation. I startle when he leans towards me, pulling me slightly by his left hand, and cups my cheeks. As he moves his face closer, I am mesmerised. I close my eyes. His face is so close to mine; I can hear him breathe. My heart begins to pound. I feel a streak of desire run down from my heart to my inner thighs. His fingers touching my neck gives me goosebumps. His hands move down from my face to my neck, my shoulders, my arms, finally landing on my hands in my lap. He pulls at my hands gently but firmly. He kisses my shoulder and his lips smoothly glide towards my right ear. I tilt my head to the left instinctively, wanting to feel his warm breath on my skin as he bites my ear gently. I can feel his every touch deep within me. I start breathing heavily and slight moans start coming out from my mouth.

    I finally notice how close he truly is when his lips find mine. They are soft and gentle, and yet powerful at the same time. I can't imagine anything possibly having more beauty than this moment. At first, it is just a soft caress of my lips but it soon turns into a more passionate kiss. His fingers start tangling in my hair, caressing my neck at the same time. I pull him even closer and realise I fit his body like a glove. His kiss is so soft, like the gentle fluttering of a butterfly's wings on my face. I know I'm falling fast under his spell, desperately craving his scent. It feels as if the universe hadn't exist before this and it won't after this—there's only him. The bristles of his stubble scratch my cheeks as he grips me even more firmly, like he wants to stop me from escaping. We are fully immersed in each other and I can feel his fullness and his warmth. I kiss him like he wants to be kissed—not as if I want to win a battle against him but like I am seeking closeness with him in one timeless, passionate moment. In that moment, it no longer feels like we are two people with distinct life stories—we have become one. For the first time since I woke up from my coma, I feel fully alive, and I have never been more grateful to be alive than I am right now. I want this moment to never end, but alas that is not to be.

'You don't remember any of this?' he asks, breaking the spell. He looks eager to know my answer. 'Because, the way you kissed me back right now, it still feels the same. Same as the very first time you kissed me and every other time after that. Your face and expressions still show the same desire. Like you want more; like you never want this moment to end.'

Can he read my mind? Or, is it that I have expressed similar feelings to him in our intimate moments earlier? How does he know? All these thoughts cross my mind as he waits for my answer. The silence increases the tension between us. His words, 'You don't remember this?' are making me feel so helpless. My eyes well up with tears.

'I am sorry, Sahil. But I don't remember anything.'

He can see the truth in my eyes and I can see the disappointment in his. He moves back to his seat and starts the car as if nothing has happened. He is silent all the way till we reach my aunt's house. I am feeling such emptiness inside me that I am unable to utter a single word. A few moments ago, we had been sharing an intense, passionate kiss, in the course of which I had felt as if our souls had united. Now, we are behaving like complete strangers.

'Thank you for coming to help me,' I tell him as he waits for a couple of seconds after I close the door. I want to say, *'Please forgive me. If you don't love me that's fine. But please don't hate me.'*

But he leaves without even looking at me, like I mean nothing to him.

The next morning in the bus, Megha sees my worn-out face and asks, 'Are you alright? Is something bothering you?' When I turn towards her and pretend to smile, she adds, 'I mean, you seem lost.'

'But I am all right,' I lie.

'Really? You know, I am your good friend, right? At least I believe so.'

'Of course,' I say.

'And I know something is troubling you. Because even if you have forgotten to tell me about your date with Rudra or have decided to keep the details a secret, there's no way you could have forgotten my birthday, unless something was wrong, right?'

Shit! Megha is right. I have been lost, thinking over and over about what had happened with Sahil last night. For a moment I consider telling her about my stalker and everything that had happened because of that. But it is her birthday. Is telling her on her birthday a good idea?

'I am so, so sorry, Megha. Wishing you a very happy birthday,' I say with a smile and hug her.

'Thank you so much, my darling.' She smiles back at me and then asks, 'So now will you tell me what's bothering you?'

I sigh. If I could tell my secret to Sahil, surely I can do the same with Megha. After all, she is my only friend. Even though Sahil has judged me for my secret, I am sure Megha wouldn't do that. We reach our destination so we get up from our seats and alight. 'Let's go to our café in the evening if you don't have any other plans?' I ask Megha.

'Of course. Why not? I want to know all about your date with Rudra.' She wiggles her eyebrows at me playfully, 'Even if you forgot my birthday.'

By now I have made up my mind to tell Megha everything. The more I keep my feelings suppressed, the more mental turmoil I am going to undergo. I need to break the barriers I have built around me.

What I hadn't been expecting though was seeing Sahil waiting by the college gate. Megha frowns when she sees him, and my conversation with him yesterday comes rushing back. He glances at me for a second and then shifts his gaze to Megha.

'Happy Birthday, Megha,' he wishes her.

'Thanks, Sahil.'

Sahil adjusts his college bag on his shoulders and says, 'Kartik wants to meet you. He told me that you haven't been answering his calls.'

Megha's face turns red in anger when she hears Kartik's name. 'I don't want to meet him. Please tell him that once and for all.'

'I am not going to come between you two. Handle it yourself,' Sahil replies and then turns to me. My heart skips a beat as our eyes meet. 'I want to talk to you.' He pauses and adds, 'Alone.'

Yesterday night, I had thought that he might never look at me again. But now he wants to be alone with me. *What is going on?* I am sure he wants to talk about yesterday. But what about yesterday? Megha leaves us alone, but not before giving me a stern stare and saying, 'I'll talk to you later. In the evening.' She would surely want to know everything about this encounter. As she leaves, her stare turns into a mischievous smile. I don't know how to react and stand there motionless. Even though Sahil and I are standing in front of each other, I try my best to avoid eye contact with him. But when he doesn't say anything for a minute, I break the silence, 'Sahil, you wanted to talk to me, right?'

He hesitates a bit before he says, 'Can we go somewhere else? We can be back before the lectures start.'

I can see he desperately wants to talk to me. I agree and he takes me to his car. As soon as I open the door, the memories of our kiss last evening flash before my eyes. I am lost in the vision of the two of us kissing passionately, until Sahil snaps a finger in front of me, bringing me back to reality. 'Shall we?'

I nod and get inside. Sahil swiftly drives us away. Nervously, I keep trying to catch glances of him from the corner of my eyes. He isn't looking as furious as he did yesterday but the anxiety on his face is clear to see. I am wondering what he could possibly want to talk about. I want to know whether he really believes me and whether he is still angry with me after knowing the truth. I'm staring at him as if staring at him long enough, might get me the answers I want.

'Don't you get tired of staring at me?' he asks, and for the first time I see a smile on his face. To see him flash that big, genuine smile gladdens my heart. It is as if the dark clouds have parted and golden sunshine is pouring down on his face. This is the right time to ask him if he believes what I had told him yesterday. I grab the opportunity and ask, 'Are you still angry with me after knowing the truth?'

'No.' There is honesty in his voice. 'I'm sorry.'

His apology surprises me. I look at him and ask, 'Why?'

'I behaved rudely with you.' He has an unexpected softness in his voice as he continues, 'I should have been kinder to you. It must not have been easy for you to keep this secret hidden for so long.'

Am I dreaming? I don't think I have ever seen this side to Sahil.

'It's okay. You don't need to be sorry.' I take a deep breath of relief, 'I deserved your wrath for hiding my condition from you for so long.'

'Anyway, I just want to apologise,' he says.

'And what about us?' I don't know how but these words instantly rush out of my mouth. Maybe I'd spent too much time last night thinking about Sahil and what would happen next. Now that he knows about my condition and even believes me, what am I supposed to do next?

He hears the stress in my voice and sees the distress on my face. 'Nandini, you don't need to worry or force yourself to remember why we broke up.'

'But you always ask me that. You clearly want to know why our relationship ended. Don't you?'

He remains silent for some time, but keeps staring at me. His gaze is so intense that I have to turn away from him. But what he says next pulls the rug right from under me.

'What if I don't want to be reminded of why our relationship ended?' he asks. 'What if I don't want you to remember why we broke up? Because the truth is I want to be with you even if it means making a fresh start.'

What?! Is he serious or is he mocking me? He wants us to be together? Again? My eyes widen in shock and my heart almost stops beating on hearing his words. He continues as if he hasn't noticed my reaction. 'I have been wrong all this time. I used to think I was the one who had suffered. But I only lost you, whereas you lost everything you ever had. I can't bring back your mother or your memories, but I can at least be with you and make you feel better.'

He caresses my cheeks as he says this. For a second, I just want to hold onto his hand and tell him that I, too, want to be with him and make memories with him again. But, in the next moment I think, what if I end up hurting him again? That thought is enough to send shivers down my spine. He sees my hesitation and continues, 'I shifted from Khajjiar to Kangra not only because I wanted to pursue college here but also because I wanted to run away from you. However, even after coming here I haven't been able to get over you. I still love you madly. I have been rude and heartless every time I have seen you lately only because I didn't want to break down in front of you. I really love you, Nandini.'

His eyes are telling me he isn't lying. For the first time since I have met him after recovering from my coma, I can see him trying to shed the hard skin he had grown to hide his emotions. But I still feel scared. I gather courage and tell him, 'You know right that I am not the same girl I used to be. I am not your old Nandini.'

He holds my hands firmly in his left hand while his right hand continues caressing my cheek and playing with my hair. The tingling sensation of his touch makes my heart beat faster. I can feel my breath becoming heavier by the second as my mind goes back to the memories of how yesterday had ended. But he smiles and pulls me closer to whisper, 'Trust me, you might have forgotten everything but you haven't forgotten yourself. I am sure of this by the way you kissed me yesterday, the way you care for everyone around you, it's all you. The old Nandini. You should embrace life once again. You deserve that because you are the best. It's time to be brave—to not just face life like you are doing right now but to also embrace it with open arms. I want you to always remember that no matter where you are in life, no matter how low you have fallen, no matter how bleak the situation seems, that is NOT THE END. This is not the end of your story. This is not the end of our story.'

It is so wonderful to hear these words. But I am still afraid to move forward. What if things don't end up in the way he wants them to? I can't stop wondering about how everything could have gone so wrong when we had been together earlier, especially after I hear Sahil's lovely words. 'I don't know what to say,' is all I manage.

'Take your own time. Don't stress yourself. I understand what you are going through. I'll be there for you. Now and forever,' he says.

It's always a battle between the heart and the mind. We don't always know which one is right and which to follow in tough situations. But I know that I cannot follow my heart because it is even more confused than my mind. My life has become one big 'I don't know' and I really don't know what to do about that.

15

Megha: Trust Me, You Are Strong Too!

Relationships end but memories last forever. And, no matter how hard you try, those memories never go away. I am looking at a photograph on my phone of Kartik and me together that we had clicked on my last birthday, when I sense a shadow has fallen over me. I realise it is Kartik standing behind me and I immediately switch off my screen. But it is too late. He has already seen me reminiscing about the moment in that picture. I take the crutch that is propped up beside me and am about to get up when he sits beside me and holds my hand.

'Don't leave. I want to talk to you,' he says.

I keep the crutch back and turn towards him, 'What is it now, Kartik? There's nothing left to say between us.'

His eyes are moist and I notice the dark circles under them. 'I don't know how to tell you this. But I should because if I don't convey it here and now, then we'll never move past this and we'll just keep silently drifting apart.'

I shut my eyes trying to control my anger for a moment and take a deep breath before I say, 'Look, Kartik, I had never expected you would treat me the way you did. Your words still echo inside my head, destroying me over and over again. How could you have demeaned me by referring to my disability as if it was my fault?' I remember his harsh words again and feel terrible all over again. It had been so insensitive of him to say that I can't be like other girls because I am not normal.

My voice quivered. 'Is it my fault that I have an atrophied leg? This is not the first time I have told you that you need to control your anger but you never take me seriously. Even if I forgive you right now, you are going to repeat the same thing again. I am sure of that.'

He sighs, 'I had never meant to do that. I hadn't even been angry. You never allowed me to explain myself. What I had meant to say was that you don't need to take up a job and add more stress to your life. I'm here to take care of you. I don't want you to overburden yourself with a job along with your studies. That's why I had said that you aren't like other girls.' His voice softens further and he adds apologetically, 'I know I should have used my words carefully and I am extremely sorry that I hurt you. Do you think we can put this behind us? Believe me, not even a thousand apologies can express how awful I feel. It hadn't been my intention to make you feel unworthy. Please let's not forget the beautiful moments we shared together.'

I am at a loss for words.

Have I actually misunderstood him all these days? Why hadn't he made his meaning clear earlier? I know that even if he had, I might not have accepted his explanation. It is only with time that I have realised his importance in life. I realise that I have not moved on from him. I still love him.

When Kartik sees the anger leaving my face, he says, 'I know you love me too. We cannot stay like this. I want you to be with me. You were right; I am indeed an idiot. But this idiot loves you beyond measure. Please let's forget what happened. I have realised that I am incomplete without you.'

I can't control my happiness. He intertwines our fingers and says, 'By the way, many happy returns of the day.'

'The day has now truly turned happy for me.' I blush and cannot stop smiling.

If we hadn't been in college right then, I might have kissed him right there. Someone has said it right. The longevity of a relationship doesn't depend on destiny but rather on the choice that two brave people make—to work on it, to fight for it and to keep at it.

After bunking most of my lectures and spending the whole day with Kartik, I meet Nandini in the evening. We reach the café almost simultaneously and order our meal as soon as we sit down. Nandini still doesn't open up to me like I am expecting her to. But her face clearly reveals that something is bothering her. After waiting for some time for her to take the initiative, I realise I've had enough and say, 'I know you are hiding something from me. Maybe you don't trust me because we have been friends only for a month. But I told you about Kartik, and opened up my heart to you. You, too, can trust me a bit, can't you?'

Nandini looks at me nervously. 'It's not about you. I am just afraid of what people will think once they get to know the truth. And hence I haven't revealed anything. To anyone.'

I look at her anxiously, 'Did you murder someone?'

'No!' She laughs.

I give her a teasing smile. 'Then, it's fine. You can tell me.'

She stares at me for a long time, probably gathering up the courage to reveal her truth to me. I am right. Finally, she starts rolling up her sleeves slowly. I'm aghast to see the scars on her arms.

'What happened to you?' I ask, horrified.

Nandini tells me about her accident and how she lost her memory because of it. It is an unbelievable incident and I am flooded with sympathy for her as I hear her story. By the end of it, tears are rolling down my cheeks. 'Why didn't you tell me about all this earlier? I thought I was the only one who was suffering.'

'Maybe I should have. But I needed time. When I spoke to you on the first day, I had seen a spark in you which gave me a lot of courage. Believe it or not, you have been a strong pillar of support for me all this while.'

I wipe off my tears and hug her tight. Now that I know everything, I feel so connected to Nandini. She, too, breaks down in tears and I put my arms around her to console her. Suddenly I remember Sahil and his strange request from the morning.

'But why did Sahil want to talk to you alone earlier? Does he know about all this?'

Nandini gives me a hesitant smile. 'I told him yesterday. After my date with Rudra, I had met Sahil.'

'What? Two dates in one day?' I am surprised.

'No, it's not that. It's complicated,' she says.

Eventually, she narrates the other half of her story and says, 'So that's it. We were in a relationship before my accident.'

I am ecstatic to hear this because I already had a sneaking suspicion about it. 'I knew it! The way he would stare at you all the time, I knew something was cooking between you. But I always thought you both must have dated in the past.' *But then why had Sahil wanted to speak to Nandini alone?* 'Oh, wait a minute, does he want to be back with you again?'

She presses her lips and nods, 'He says he still loves me. But I don't know what to do.'

'Are you crazy?' I am surprised. How can she not know what to do? Isn't it pretty obvious? 'Even after such a long time he is in love with you. You must be foolish and blind if you can't see that in his eyes.'

Nandini considers my words carefully. She knows I am not wrong. I continue, 'Despite knowing nothing about your accident, he has continued to love you. Don't waste your time thinking about the past. Go, be with him now so that later you don't look back at this time and regret the choices you have made.'

'But what if ...' Nandini tries to say something but I interrupt her. 'Don't think too much, Nandini. You don't want to live with regrets. I, too, accepted Kartik's apology today when he said he was sorry for what he had done. That's because I don't want to have any regrets about our relationship.'

'What ... really? You guys are back together?' She clearly hadn't seen that coming and is completely astonished.

'Yes, and I want you and Sahil to be together too. You both look cute together. Like you are made for each other. So, get over those traumatic memories and accept what's waiting for you.' I hold her hand and look into her eyes, 'Like your mother, you are a strong woman too.'

No one is perfect. Life is messy, relationships are complex and outcomes are uncertain. But when a person truly loves you, they accept your past, support you in the present and want to be with you through thick and thin in the future. I really wish she agrees to be with Sahil again.

16

Nandini: I Love You

The morning is still dark, and standing in the mist, I feel enveloped by a blanket of stillness. I am at the Bajreshwari temple—the temple of the goddess in whom, I had been told, my mother had immense faith. The clouds are flashing with some lightning but the wind has stilled. I feel my mother's strong presence around me. There may be some people who won't believe me when I say that, but others who have experienced something similar will agree with me. It isn't something I can explain in words. The sensation is unnatural, like a force is trying to grab hold of me, trying to make its presence felt. I should be crying right now, but I am strangely calm. Maasi had told me how attached my mother had been to this temple, so being here is the only way I can think of, to understand what is happening with me. Maasi and I take the goddess's blessings and then, she takes me to the place in the premises where Mom's religious group would offer their prayers and help kids who were begging nearby.

I can see the name of the group carved on the huge marble stone in front of us.

Bajreshwari Mata Bhakti Sthaan.

The names of all the trustees are also carved on the marble. I skim through them and find my mother's name.

Asha Kashyap.

A sense of calm comes over me and I close my eyes. Next to me, I hear Maasi say, 'Oh God, I hope wherever Asha is, she is happy to see her daughter getting back to what she once was.'

I can still feel the force of my mother around me. Am I hallucinating or is this real? It is a strange feeling because I have never experienced such a thing before. I don't share that thought with Maasi, but I close my eyes and join my hands to pray for my mother's salvation. 'Ma, I love you. I miss you. I know you are still around me.'

It's difficult to define your relationship with your mother, isn't it? I had thought that if I acknowledged that here, the force around me would intensify and I'd know it is related to my mother. But nothing of that sort happens. Maybe it is just my love for my mother. I had so desperately wanted to feel like she was around me. However, my words trigger Maasi's emotions and her loss. She breaks down into tears, saying how much she misses her sister.

'I am sorry, Ma,' I whisper in a voice low enough for Maasi not to hear.

I am sorry for having forgotten her and our memories together, for forgetting everything related to us. I wish I would be able to recollect them someday so that I can know how much she loved me.

Dear Ma, please know that you are missed. Your absence is felt every day of my life since you were stolen from me. I can never forget you. A part of me is still lost and I am wondering if I will ever get it back. Maybe that piece is in heaven with you and someday you can put it back in me and I will be whole again.

That evening, I take special permission from Maasi to go to Megha's birthday party. Megha doesn't drink alcohol on her birthday and thus, always organises her party on the day after her birthday. It's a double celebration because she is now back with Kartik. He, too, is going to be at the party along with Sahil. I am nervous about seeing Sahil again and have even considered staying home to avoid meeting him. But that would be unfair to Megha. Megha wants me to have a word with Sahil and I have agreed because there is no point in dragging this matter when there are no secrets between us anymore.

My mind is occupied with these thoughts on the drive to the venue—a lounge on the other side of town—and before I realise it, I have reached. I am clearly the first one to reach, so I text Megha.

How much time? I have reached.

Megha replies instantly.

Oh, you've already reached. Sahil was supposed to pick us up. Sorry, I forgot to tell you. Anyway, we will reach in 30 minutes.

Damn, 30 more minutes. I enter the lounge, hoping to wait for them inside. But the music is on full blast and is hurting my ears. Dozens of people are dancing to the music. I can see couples making out in the corners and on the couches as if they are the only ones around. It is better to wait for Megha and others outside. I am about to step out when, suddenly, a hand grabs my wrist. I turn expecting to see Sahil, but it is Rudra instead.

'Nandini, what are you doing here?' He is smiling as if he is happy to see me. Before I can say anything, he continues, 'Come along. My friends are here. You might not know them, but they definitely know you.' He smiles some more. 'Of course, because of me.'

But—I dither.

If Sahil sees me with Rudra again, it will only make the situation worse. After all this time, things have finally become better between Sahil and me, and I don't want to spoil it. But Rudra isn't paying any attention to my protests and he pulls me towards his group quickly. I turn to see if Megha and the boys have arrived, but they are nowhere in sight. I am relieved and quickly greet Rudra's friends before making an excuse to leave. 'I need to go to the washroom,' I say and make my exit.

I walk away feeling as if I have won a battle. I surely would have to explain myself if Sahil spotted us together, that too only one day after his proposal. But my feeling of victory is premature because I soon realise I haven't won yet. As I am about to enter the washroom, Rudra pulls me roughly towards him. *He followed me!* As I look into his eyes for the first time that evening, I realise he is utterly drunk, and has, maybe, even consumed some drugs. Suddenly, the image of the stalker from a couple of days ago flashes in front of my eyes. Had it been Rudra? I am not sure. He comes closer and I can smell the alcohol on his breath.

In a slurred tone, he asks, 'Where are you going?'

I feel disgusted with myself for having gone out on a date with this guy. I had thought he was a sweet, innocent guy but now, I am reminded of Megha's warnings. She had been right all along.

'What are you doing? Let go of me,' I say firmly. I try to push him away but Rudra's grip on my wrist is too strong. I look to my left and right, hoping to ask someone for help. But all I can see in the passage are people engrossed in kissing each other. In fact, with the lights so dim, even Rudra and I might look like a kissing couple if someone isn't paying close attention.

But Rudra is being very aggressive with me. 'Why are you feeling afraid? We even went on a date. So, what's the problem? Am I not your type?'

The look of lust in his eyes is scaring the hell out of me. 'Please leave me, you are drunk.'

'It's fun to kiss someone once you are doped.' He comes closer as if he wants to smell me. 'Especially if the girl is as hot as you. Look at you, your figure ...' He scans me lewdly from head to toe and I shudder.

'My perception of you was all wrong,' I shout at him.

As soon as he hears my words, he loses control and pulls me towards him by my waist. He tries to force his lips on mine but I scream, 'Rudra, stop this.'

That's when people around us stop doing whatever they had been doing and start staring at us. Even then, no one comes to my rescue. Suddenly, I hear Megha's voice. She is calling out to Sahil, asking him to come quickly. I can't describe the relief I feel when I see Sahil. He looks at Rudra with his one hand pressed against mine and the other one grabbing my waist. A murderous look takes over his face, and he runs towards us, pulling Rudra away from me and punching his face. After a couple of blows, Rudra falls to the ground but Sahil doesn't stop there. He keeps kicking him again and again, until Kartik manages to pull him away.

Angrily, Sahil frees himself from Kartik's grip and yells at Rudra. 'Don't you ever come close to her again. Or even try to talk to her. I swear I'll beat the hell out of you!' He kicks Rudra hard one more time and shouts, 'Next time, you wouldn't even be able to stand on your feet.'

Sahil grabs my hand and leads me out of the lounge. Kartik and Megha follow. They can see I am still terrified.

Megha rubs my back and gently, tells me to calm down. 'Chill, baby, nothing happened. We are here with you.'

My entire body is trembling and when Sahil puts his hand on my shoulder, I embrace him tightly without a second thought. In no time, my body relaxes and the tension leaves me. Sahil's warmth has calmed me down. I feel so secure in his arms. I don't know how long I cling to Sahil. I release him only when Megha suggests to him, 'Take her home, Sahil. We'll catch up some other time.'

Sahil nods and we get inside his car. We don't exchange a single word but I can feel his anger radiating off him. He is furious because he hadn't liked my closeness with Rudra even earlier. Now, after this incident, he doesn't want me to talk to Rudra either. It is only once we drive away in darkness that he breaks the silence.

'Did he hurt you?' Sahil's eyes are fixed on the road ahead. He still looks angry enough to kill Rudra.

'No.'

He shakes his head and asks, 'Why the fuck do you like being around Rudra? Whenever I see you with him, my blood starts to boil. Not because I am jealous, but because I know what a creep that guy is.'

'I don't know ... I should've kept my distance,' I mutter in an apologetic tone.

I am still battling my inner fears, wondering what would have happened if Sahil, Megha and Kartik hadn't reached in time.

He presses his palm to my cheek and gives me a comforting look. 'Don't worry, he'll never harass you again.'

I believe him. I love how much he cares for me. I love how relieved I feel in his arms. I love how secure I feel by his touch.

I lean towards him. I am now more certain than ever that I used to love him before my accident. I move closer to him and express my innermost thoughts. 'Make me fall in love with you, Sahil. Once more,' I say.

He looks completely shocked. He speaks, as if he is in a dream, 'What did you say? You mean, your answer is, yes?'

For the first time since I can remember, I am not confused. My eyes reflect my love for him. There's a brand-new sensation in my heart. I can't understand what is happening to me but, as they say, you feel this way when you are in love. I want to explore these feelings with Sahil, 'Yes, make me yours, Sahil. And this time for forever. You know me better than a lot of people. I can't help but be honest with you. Every time I'm around you, I feel like I'm being pulled towards you. I wasn't strong enough to fight my feelings for you earlier but, to be honest, I am thankful that I wasn't.'

His face starts glowing and he gives me a smile that can power someone through their worst storms. I have already forgotten what had happened with Rudra. I wanted us to throw away all our sorrows and pain, and reclaim our long-lost love.

Sahil has a mischievous smile on his face, 'You know ... I can never get enough of you. If you were ever convicted of a crime, I'd be the person leading your defence. I don't know what souls are made of, but yours and mine are made of the same thing.'

His words make me blush. I have felt imprisoned for a year now, but Sahil's love has broken down the cage and released my soul. Hopefully, we can now go into the future together and unscramble the puzzle that is incomplete without the other. I feel happy, I feel content in his arms! I want to start afresh. I want to learn to love again. I want to love him all over again.

17

Nandini: No One Can Replace You

It's an amazing feeling when someone new comes into your life, someone from whom you had no expectations, and then out of nowhere, right in front of you, they become everything you ever needed. I have firmly turned away from my past and opened my heart to new beginnings. After Sahil had dropped me home yesterday, after that awful incident with Rudra, he had called me and we'd chatted over the phone for hours. I feel as if a new soul has entered my body. However, I must admit that we are both unsure about how to take things forward even though we have decided to be in a relationship. I am worried about hurting Sahil again and he has to deal with the bitter feelings that had arisen in him in the aftermath of my accident. But we are both determined to weather any storm, and that is all that matters.

The next day when I meet Megha at the bus stop, I cannot stop smiling because Sahil and I are together again. She reciprocates with the same excitement and delight.

'I am so happy for you and Sahil. You both look really cute together. Everyone in college will be jealous of you.'

My cheeks turn red; I have lost count of how many times I have blushed in the last few hours. But when Megha speaks about other people in our college, I remember Rashi. How will she react when she comes to know about us? The smile that has been plastered on my face since yesterday suddenly fades. As we walk in through the college gates, I see Kartik waiting for us. He greets Megha with a hug and turns towards me. 'How are you feeling now?' he asks.

'I am good,' I nod, smiling gently.

'Of course, you'll be good. Now that you are in love again. Aren't you?' he says, teasingly.

'You're right.' I look down shyly for a second and then glance up again. 'But I didn't get a chance to thank you. For yesterday,' I say.

'Oh, you don't need to. I am glad the situation didn't become worse.'

We are chit-chatting casually when Sahil arrives. He has a surprise for me. He and I are going on a date.

Our first official date!

Sahil takes me to a hilltop café in Bir village which is an hour away from Kangra. I love the place; its vibrant colours and the dim illumination of fairy lights gives the café a romantic vibe. I am overjoyed and tell Sahil as much. 'I love the place. This feels surreal.'

'I knew you'd like it.' He holds my waist and pulls me closer as we sit on the table. 'You always loved such places.' His lips widen into a breath-taking smile, a smile I absolutely adore. I love the fact that Sahil still remembers my likes and dislikes, even though I can't. We order baked beans and apple cinnamon cake along with some momos.

Sahil excuses himself for a minute and returns with a gift in his hand. Just when I thought our date couldn't get any better, he has managed to surprise me again.

'Wow, what is that? It looks huge,' I say as he hands me the gift and kisses my cheek.

'Don't open it now,' he requests and whispers in my ears, 'But I am sure you will love it. It's something you have always loved.'

I am sure I will. He keeps his elbows on the table and rests his chin on his hands. 'Are you real, Nandini?' he asks. His eyes refuse to look anywhere else but at me.

'What do you mean? Of course, I am,' I say, surprised.

'Sometimes ...' he sighs, 'I feel as if this is all a dream.'

He is afraid that I will vanish again. But I poke his cheek with my index finger and say, 'See, I am real.'

At that, his face breaks into a smile. A server interrupts our conversation and places our order on the table. The food looks delicious.

'Wow, it's heavenly,' I say, taking a bite of the momo.

'You haven't seen heavenly yet.' He winks, biting the other half of the momo in my mouth.

'Shut up.' I teasingly punch his chest. As we continue eating, I say, 'I want to know more about you.' I glance up to see that my question has caught him off guard. 'I mean, you know everything about me, but I don't remember ...'

The expression on his face changes as he suddenly remembers that I have no memory of the past. 'Okay, go on.'

I clear my throat and start, 'How many people are there in your family?'

'Me, my mom and my dad.'

'You said that you moved here because of me. Is that true?' I ask hesitantly.

'Completely true. But my dad doesn't know the real reason for my move. He believes I wanted to shift so that I could attend a good college. But Khajjiar was too much for me to handle.' He takes a deep breath and continues, 'Everything about that place would remind me of you.'

'I am sorry.' I look down in remorse.

But he startles me by kissing my cheek. I love how he can cheer me up every time I am sad. We continue our Q&A session for some more time until I wrap it up with one last question.

'I don't know why I left you in the first place, but I'm not going to leave you again, Sahil. Unless ... you cheated on me last time?'

My question offends him so much that he looks aghast. 'I didn't. Even your mother knew about our relationship. Why would I do that?'

'Sssh!' I put my fingers on his lips to calm him down. 'I was just teasing you.'

I am in love with every moment that I spend with him and in those moments, he is everything that I had ever wanted and hoped for. Our entire day together passes by in a blink. While returning, Sahil chooses a deserted road and stops the car in a secluded spot. The moment becomes even more romantic with the dark and quiet that surrounds us. I turn to look at him; his skin is glowing in the dim light that falls on us from the streetlight. The night is serene; the sunlight from the day has warmed the atmosphere but a slight breeze plays with my hair. We have stopped on a narrow, isolated road that is probably not in use a lot. I close the black, tinted windows of his car and turn my gaze back at him. Sahil looks unsure of making the first move; he is waiting for my approval. He moves closer to me. I offer no objection but the confused look on his face remains. Is he wondering if my silence means I am scared or not ready to take the next step. But when I respond by touching his arm and leaning towards him, Sahil smiles.

'Do you want to take our relationship forward?' he whispers closer to my ear.

'Yes, I want to feel you,' I answer. He moves towards my neck and lets out a low breath, tickling me in the process, creating sensations I don't think I've ever felt before.

He leans further into me, lingering for a moment on my lips before finally lifting his head to meet my eyes. He immediately covers my mouth with his, his lips touching mine, slowly caressing them and withdrawing again and again. I am instantly aroused. I can feel our breaths merge and our bodies becoming warm. I make soft sounds to convey my pleasure, my excitement. Sahil continues kissing me gently, carefully. But I don't want gentleness today. He caresses my hair, nibbles along my ear lobes and softly whispers, 'You feel so good. I want you to take me to heaven.'

We quickly move to the back seat of the car to be more comfortable. We know we don't have much time and want to make the most of it. I instantly rip open his shirt while he takes my top off. His fingers slowly trail down my skin. I pull him closer, burying my nails in his back. The low height of the seat and the way I am leaning back has created the perfect position.

'Someone's a little too eager,' Sahil rasps as he breathes against my neck.

I can sense that he wouldn't be able to hold back for too long, and I moan in pleasure at the thought. My fingers lock around his neck, my breath is on his face. I tease him with my fingertips as he begins to stroke the length of my body with his. I put my lips against his ear, whispering his name over and over, like a chant, making him gasp.

He is slow and gentle with me at first. But we are soon overcome with desire and Sahil enters me. I moan as I feel a sharp, acute pain. 'Sssh ... it's all right, don't worry, just relax,' he says.

I cannot get enough of him. I want him to squeeze into me further and further. I want to watch him fall apart, so that I never forget this moment. He knows my body so well and I hum with pleasure as he touches me everywhere. There is no more pain. Just pleasure. Incredible pleasure. Like the universe doesn't exist; like only the two of us exist. I don't want the night to come to an end. My moans get louder with each drop of sweat tickling my skin. I hold on to him as I reach my climax. I can feel the car rocking, as we draw closer together, until Sahil reaches his peak too. He gives me a huge smile of satisfaction; I'm sure my expression mirrors his.

'Was it how you had imagined it?' he asks.

'So much more. I love you,' I reply. I am so happy, I can announce it to the whole world.

We hadn't made love; we had felt love!

'Call me later?' Sahil asks as I get off the car at Maasi's house.

I don't like speaking over the phone; I prefer texting to calling. I probably wasn't like this before the accident because

Sahil insists on talking on the phone. I find talking on the phone boring but since it makes Sahil happy, I say, 'Sure.'

Sahil waits until I have entered the main gate. Both of us are still worried about the stalker from the other night, who I now suspect could be Rudra. These little moments show that Sahil truly cares about me. I feel so happy knowing that. I wave at him and go inside the house. But as soon as I shut the door behind me, I sense that something isn't right. I hear loud voices coming from Maasi's bedroom.

Are they fighting again? Or has Rashi done something? I look in the direction of Rashi's room; her door is open which means she still hasn't come home. I take a step closer to Maasi and uncle's room and hear Maasi's voice. 'Anil, what are we supposed to do? I am sure he will come back for her again. He looked obsessed.'

Maasi is sounding panicked. The door is ajar and I can see Uncle is patting Maasi's back to calm her down. 'Just relax,' he tells her. 'We will call the cops next time. Don't worry.'

'You don't understand, do you? The cops can't do anything. You know that.'

A terrible feeling has gripped me and I start shivering, wondering who it is they are talking about. I rush inside the room to see Maasi crying.

'Is everything all right?' I ask. Maasi is sitting on the edge of the bed and Uncle is standing in front of her, consoling her. 'Why are you crying?' I ask.

She turns to see my worried face and then turns back to Uncle. They stare at each other without saying a word. They certainly weren't expecting me to hear their conversation. Maasi doesn't move for a while and keeps glancing at me and

Uncle alternately. Eventually, she stands up and walks up to me. She clasps my hand and sits me down on the bed. Then, she holds me by my shoulders and says, 'We need to talk.' She looks frightened and my mind starts racing, thinking of all the worst-case scenarios that could have happened. But I don't say anything and wait for her to speak. Every second that she stays silent makes my heart pound even more, almost as if it is trying to break free from my ribs.

'I can't believe it's really happening, but sadly it is.'

She again takes a hauntingly long pause. I can't bear it anymore and say tersely, 'Just tell me please. You are scaring me now.'

'Look, when you were in a coma, a lot of things happened,' Maasi says, gathering her courage as she wipes her tears. 'Asha's death was one thing. And the threat to your life was another.'

I begin to feel numb. 'What do you mean?'

'So ...' She looks momentarily at Uncle and then turns back to me when he nods at her. 'So, after Asha's death, I had decided that you will stay with us. I felt you were my responsibility. By taking care of you, I wanted to assuage the guilt I was feeling and make sure that your mother's soul could rest in peace. But now, your father has come back and wants to take you away with him.'

I am dumbfounded. My hands and legs start trembling in disbelief. My vision blurs and my mind stops working once I fully understand her words. Why is he back all of a sudden after so many years? The image of the stalker flashes in my head again.

Had it actually been my father and not Rudra?

Maasi had said that he had left us before I was born. I have no memory of him, but I'm curious about him. I feel like seeing him, meeting him, to ask him why he left and now why he is back.

Will I finally get to meet my father? What does he want with me? Is he really the way Maasi had described him?

There are too many thoughts racing through my mind right now.

Did I want to meet him because I had lost my mother and he was the only parent I had left? Would I have felt the same way even before the accident, knowing that he hadn't tried to be a part of my life in my growing years?

'But why is he back?' I ask, keeping all my feelings aside.

Uncle steps into the conversation now. 'That's what we don't know. We have given it a lot of thought, but we still have no concrete answers.'

'I am sure there must be some bloody political reason behind it,' Maasi shouts angrily.

'What?' I can't understand what she means.

'Your father is a shrewd businessman from Delhi,' Maasi reveals. Before this, I'd had no idea what my father did for a living. Even Sahil hadn't mentioned anything to me. Maybe Mom had never told me anything about him because he never existed for us. 'He comes from an influential, wealthy family and that's why he hadn't been able to go against his father. He left your mother and you alone, so she left Delhi and moved to Khajjiar where our parents used to live once.'

I feel a sudden dread and a sense of coldness starts taking over me, making me feel numb. I feel as if my world is crumbling around me. Maasi is saying something to uncle but I can't hear her because of all the voices in my head. It is only when uncle shakes me vigorously that I hear him say, 'Don't worry, we will handle him.'

'But what if he comes back when I am alone at home?'

Even the thought enrages Maasi. 'I will kill that bastard. I'll not let him take you along with him. Never!' Maasi declares.

Ever since Maasi had told me that my father had abandoned my mother and me, I hadn't considered him a part of my family. I had come to accept that both my mother and father were dead. That was the only truth I knew. But now that my father was back in town, why were my thoughts veering towards him?

What was his motive in returning to Kangra? And how can he think he can return and become a part of my life whenever he wants?

I feel an ache deep within my heart. In a place that is occupied by anger, confusion and pain. Just when I had thought my life was becoming normal again, my father reappears. Just when I had started imagining a happy life with Sahil, my father is here to snatch it all away.

No! I won't let him do that. Not when I have just found solace in Sahil's arms.

18

Nandini: She'll Never Accept

Being in love is an all-consuming experience. It is exciting, thrilling and a little terrifying to fall head over heels in love with someone. I have realised that the passion between two people who deeply love each other burns like a wildfire. We only have eyes for each other, and everything else fades in the background. It has been just two days since Sahil and I became a couple (again) and we already have people rolling their eyes at us. I have kept a low profile since I've come to live with Maasi. But now things are out of my control. Everyone knows what had happened the evening of Megha's birthday at the lounge. I suppose one of Rudra's friends has spread the gossip. Since that day, I have been receiving odd glances from people in college. People start whispering as soon as I pass them by. I hate it! The stares make me feel as if I am to blame that Sahil and Rudra had fought. I am sure none of these people know the true reason behind the fight. Rashi must have heard about the incident as well because she bumps against my shoulder rudely as she walks past me. My bag falls to the floor. I bend down to pick it up and meet her furious eyes.

'Walk carefully,' I say firmly, raising my eyebrows.

After our heated argument at home the other day, I have decided to stop being passive in my arguments with Rashi. I have stopped thinking that Maasi is doing me a favour by taking my side. Now I know that Maasi believes in me and has chosen to stand by the person who is in the right.

'You be careful, you bitch,' Rashi almost shouts as she inches closer to me to appear even more threatening.

'Come again?' I narrow my eyes at her. I refuse to take a step back and stand there holding my ground even though she is hovering very close to me.

'You heard me. Be careful of what you do or you will regret it,' she repeats.

'Do what you want, I don't care! You're full of lies and I'm not afraid of you.'

She presses her lips tightly on hearing my words and looks as if she is about to hit me when Sahil appears from around the corner.

'Rashi, what the fuck are you doing?' He pushes her away slightly in an attempt to put some distance between us.

'Why are you doing this to me?' Her voice softens, seeing him and her eyes moisten. 'I have been calling you for the last couple of days. Why aren't you answering my calls?'

'Because I was with Nandini.' Sahil turns towards me, and intertwines his fingers with mine. He softly asks me to relax and then turns back to Rashi, 'Don't you get it? She's my girlfriend.'

'What? This bitch?' Rashi says in disbelief.

'Mind your tongue, Rashi,' Sahil raises his voice, 'She's your sister, in case you have forgotten.'

'I don't care. I'll never care,' Rashi almost screams. 'What about us?'

'What about us?' Sahil repeats her question.

'Aren't we supposed to be together?' Tears roll down her cheeks as she says this. I can see she is heartbroken.

'Have you lost it? We were never supposed to be together.' Sahil is quite stern with her, and before she can respond, he pulls at my hand and we walk away.

Here's another reason for people to pay even more attention to me. I won't be surprised if people start calling me an attention seeker. In just two days, Sahil has picked a fight with two people associated with me. I stare at Sahil as he pulls me along.

He turns around and asks, 'You okay?'

'Yes,' I nod. I want to discuss something with him and stop him.

'What happened?' he asks.

'I do not like the way you are fighting with everyone for me—one by one. First Rudra and now Rashi,' I say.

He smiles, 'I don't care if I have to fight with the rest of this world if it means being with you. I can't risk losing you again.'

I have no words to respond to that, even though my heart starts singing. I can never understand why it is so hard for me to find the right words to say to him. He always seems to take my breath away and I can't explain the fluttering feeling in my chest when he is around me. My once empty heart has been filled with his love. When he is with me, I am convinced that nothing can go wrong.

'Meet me after college?' he suggests and takes a pause before adding, 'I need to take you home.'

'Home? Why?' I am taken aback. Goosebumps break out all over my body at the thought of meeting his parents.

'Mom wants to meet you,' he says with a broad smile. 'She's been wanting to meet you ever since she got to know that we are together again.'

I am startled by his revelation. His smile suggests that it isn't the first time I'll be meeting his mom. He had said yesterday that even my mother had been aware of our relationship. Had my mother liked Sahil?

While I am excited to meet Sahil's mother, I am nervous too. I have no memory of her. 'What will I say to her? Sorry, but I can't remember even a single thing about you?'

Sahil pulls my cheeks and says laughingly, 'Why is it that you are so innocent?' Then he adds thoughtfully, 'I have told her about what you have been through. I hope you're okay with that. She's just concerned about you.'

I can think of no reason to refuse meeting his mother, so I agree. 'Okay, we'll go after college.'

He walks me to my class and leaves. As I take my seat, I ponder about how Sahil is being so open about acknowledging our relationship to the world, while I am still holding things back from him like my father's reappearance in my life. Last night, we had spent hours texting with each other, but I hadn't wanted to spoil the mood by telling him that my father was back. I had decided that I would tell him later, when the time was right.

I walk out of my classroom once my classes for the day are over. I am so lost in my own thoughts that I don't even realise when I bump into someone. I look up and see Rudra standing just outside my classroom. I am immediately wary and start looking around, hoping for Sahil to be there, but he isn't.

'I want to talk to you,' he says.

'But I don't want to talk to you,' I reply and started walking away from him.

'I am sorry for what I did; I was high.' He pauses as I turn back to look at him. 'On drugs. Forgive me,' he says.

'And how many girls have you apologised to for this exact reason?'

I can see the remorse on his face but his tone is far from genuine. 'Trust me, I am not that kind of a guy,' he says. But I am finding it hard to believe him.

I ignore him and start walking away to avoid more stares from the people around us. But I can still hear him when he shouts, 'I know you won't believe me but you are walking on fire. Sahil is not the right person for you. He's not protecting you; he's dangerous.'

Even though I don't trust Rudra, his words spark a note of fear in me. These days I am so unsure of everything that for a moment I get suspicious. *Is Rudra being truthful?* But Sahil had just said that he would fight with the world to be with me. Of course, he is protecting me, our love, our relationship. I quickly brush away the traitorous thought, telling myself that there is no reason to doubt Sahil. Ignoring Rudra's statement, I start walking towards the parking lot where Sahil has told me he will be waiting. On the way, I stop by the washroom to freshen up before meeting Sahil's mother. But as soon as I enter, I am left stunned. On the mirror, written in bold letters, are the words:

NANDINI IS A SLUT.

My eyes well up as soon as I see this. *Why can't I seem to catch a break?* There is something dramatic that happens to me every day—first the encounter with Rudra, then the news about my father and now this. I don't understand why everyone is making so much of a fuss about my relationship with Sahil. I am sure Rashi is the culprit again; this is typical behaviour for her, and she has retaliated in a similar way earlier also when she hasn't got her way.

I should have filed a complaint against her the last time she had written all those nasty things on the college wall. I quickly wipe off the words with some tissue paper and run out towards the parking lot. I decide that I won't tell Sahil about this. Unless he finds out through someone, I am keeping this to myself. Sahil is leaning against his car. I stop running and stand in my place just looking at him.

Rudra's words come back to me: 'You are walking on fire. Sahil is dangerous.' *Why would Rudra say such a thing? Is what he was saying true? Is that why I had broken up with him last time? Who is Sahil Avasthi?*

I shake myself out of my reverie. *Why am I taking Rudra's words seriously? He is the one who had actually tried to molest me. He was the dangerous one. How can I not trust Sahil who loves me so much? What if Rudra is lying to me, trying to ruin my relationship with Sahil?*

19

Nandini: Felt Like Home

When Sahil sees me approaching, he opens the car door with a smile. It disappears the minute he sees the expression on my face.

'What's wrong?' he asks, holding me by my shoulders.

I remain silent and shake my head to say that nothing's wrong. But Sahil immediately reads my mind. 'Did Rudra do something again?'

'He apologised to me,' I reveal as I meet Sahil's eyes. 'He also said that you are the wrong person for me and I should be careful,' I blurt out. On hearing this, Sahil's worried expression turns to one of fury.

'I wish I had killed him that day.' Sahil's eyes are blazing now. He looks in the direction of the college campus, his eyes searching for Rudra, and shouts, 'He'll talk rubbish and you'll take him seriously? Is this some kind of a joke?'

'I haven't taken him seriously, Sahil,' I say as I pull him towards the driver's side. 'Just calm down. We should leave now.'

Sahil doesn't argue any further and gets into the car. But he has a death grip on the steering wheel—a definite sign that he is still fuming. I wait for him to say something.

'You really believe what Rudra said?' he asks shooting a furious sideways glance at me. His question makes it seem as if he wants validation from me. For a second, I am confused. *Is he seeking validation because Rudra is right about him hiding something from me or is he genuinely asking me this out of concern?*

'Why is it so important? Just forget it,' I say in response.

'No!' His commanding voice silences me. He is quiet for a while as he continues to drive, but finally says, 'It is important. To me. For us. I want to know whether you still trust me, whether you still have faith in my love and this relationship.'

I sigh. 'I love you and I trust you.' I lean towards him and kiss his left cheek. The anger immediately leaves Sahil's face and he looks like a kid who has just been given free candy. 'Moreover, why are we even discussing Rudra when I am about to meet your mother. I am already nervous thinking about how I am supposed to act and what I am supposed to say to her,' I add.

Sahil's good mood is back. 'You must have seen the movie *Kabhi Khushi Kabhie Ghum*. You need to touch her feet and act like a *sanskari* girl,' he tells me.

'I don't remember having watched it, but I can tell by looking at your face that you're making fun of me,' I laugh.

He chuckles as he turns his gaze to the road and starts singing along with the music playing in the car. After a few minutes, I speak again, 'I'll not lie, I am really nervous about meeting your mom.'

He wraps his left arm around my neck and starts caressing my cheek. 'Stop thinking so much. She isn't going to ask you to marry me right away.'

'Stop making fun of me. I am serious,' I gently slap his hand away.

'I am serious, too. You are meeting her for the first time, but she has met you before. She knows who you are.' He stops the car and says, 'We have reached.'

Sahil is right. Even though I may not have any memories of people I met before my accident, but those people have memories of me, they would know who I am. This thought is meant to comfort me. But it still doesn't ease my tension. I scan the exterior of the house as Sahil parks the car. The veranda is extremely picturesque and much bigger than the one at Maasi's house. Its grey colour is soothing to the eyes. A few chirping birds and the gentle tinkle of the wind chime add to the sense of calm. There are colourful flowers planted along the fence and some herbs are growing on its side. A symmetric stone walkway leads up to the house. Everything is so beautiful. The soothing vibe of the house somehow eases my gloomy thoughts.

'Shall we?' Sahil pats my back, seeing me stare at the house.

'Your house is beautiful,' I tell him.

'Thanks,' he smiles. 'My mom takes care of everything here.'

I imagine his mother as someone classy and elegant. I wonder if she has forgiven me for breaking up with her son earlier.

Sahil rings the doorbell and a woman in a salwar-kameez opens the door. I immediately notice that she is shorter than I am and her skin is glowing. Her elegant platinum necklace catches my attention. I had been right about her: she is classy and elegant.

'How are you, Nandini?' she asks. She must sense some of my nervousness as my fingers keep playing with the straps of my bag. 'I heard about your accident and the amnesia. Are you feeling better now?'

'I am better, aunty. Thanks for asking.' I give her a beaming smile.

She invites me in and makes space for me on the sofa. 'Don't mind the usual daily mess. I was about to iron clothes, thinking you guys might be late.'

'It's fine, I am comfortable.' The sofa is huge and could have accommodated more than half a dozen people.

Sahil sniffs and asks his mother, 'You're cooking something?'

'Yes, I am making tikki and some chicken. Are you guys hungry?' She gets up and walks towards the kitchen. 'Nandini, you still eat chicken, right? I have made your favourite—wings.'

'Yes ...' I answer, trying to recollect if I have ever eaten chicken wings prepared by her. But nothing clicks. I hear vessels clanking in the kitchen and ask, 'Aunty, do you want some help?'

'No, I am fine. Why don't you guys freshen up? I'll set the table till then,' she replies.

Sahil shifts closer to me and gives me a small peck on my cheek. Pulling me towards him, he says teasingly, 'My bedroom is that way. Do you want to freshen up?'

I kick Sahil and push him away. 'Shut up. Don't start all this here.' I adjust my clothes and quickly look in the direction of the kitchen to make sure his mother hasn't seen us.

'It's not the first time we've done this here while she has been in the kitchen.'

'What?' I can't believe what he is saying and lean towards him to close his mouth with my palm so that his voice isn't audible to her. 'You are crazy. I don't want to hear any more details.'

Had he been serious? Had I ever been that gutsy? Maybe I had been, considering what happened in the car a few days ago.

I get up and go to Sahil's room, and he quietly follows me. We clean up in the washroom and come out to sit at the dining table. Sahil's mom serves us the food she has made and all of it looks delicious. I tell her that.

Sahil has a bite and makes a weird face. 'Too much salt. Like always.'

I give him a kick under the table for not appreciating his mother's efforts. His mother looks at me in anticipation as I take a bite.

'It's really good. Don't believe what Sahil says,' I tell her.

Sahil laughs thinking that I am saying all this just to please her, but I genuinely like the tikki and the wings that she had made.

'He is an idiot. Have some more,' she says as she serves me.

I am eagerly eating, when I suddenly feel Sahil nudging my foot underneath the table.

Oh no, not in front of his mom!

He gives me a wicked smile, but I tuck my legs under my chair.

'Mom, I am done eating. I'll change my clothes and come quickly,' he says.

When he leaves, an awkward silence sits between aunty and me, until she says, 'You know I hadn't been very pleased when I found out you had disappeared. But knowing Asha, I was sure she wouldn't leave without informing anyone unless there was a strong reason to do so.'

'You knew my mother?' I ask curiously, wanting to know more.

'Yes, we used to live near each other. I had met her a few times, but when you and Sahil started getting closer, our meetings increased. She was an exceptionally compassionate person and her world used to revolve around you.' She pauses and then holds my hand. 'I wonder how you dealt with everything alone. But now if you need anything, don't hesitate to come here. Consider this your own home.'

I'm still struck by what she said earlier. *Why had Mom wanted to leave the city overnight? Even Maasi had mentioned the same thing and now Sahil's mom had repeated that my mother wouldn't leave without informing anyone unless there was a strong reason. But what had been that strong reason?*

I am still thinking about all this when I get up to wash my hands. Suddenly, an image flashes in front of my eyes.

Sahil's mother and my mom sitting and chatting at a dining table in a huge room with two partitions, similar to this one. There are a couple of other women around, too, but their faces are blurred. I can hear their voices. Beyond the partition, Sahil and I are sitting on a sofa and watching a movie on the television. Sahil's mom gets up to go to the kitchen, when she comes to our side of the room. She sees Sahil and me holding hands. We are so engrossed in the movie that we haven't seen her come in. As soon as she sees us, she starts screaming at us.

'Nandini,' Sahil shouts from the bedroom, and I snap back to the present. He comes out and says, 'Come inside, I want to show you something.'

I follow him, glancing towards his mom as I go. She is cleaning the mess in the kitchen and doesn't seem to notice us going inside the room. Maybe Sahil had been right. Maybe we had been in his room together earlier as well while his mother had been outside. But I'm troubled by what I had seen in my flashback—in that memory his mother had clearly been extremely upset to see Sahil and me holding hands.

Sahil pulls me inside and slams the door shut. I am scared. What if his mother screams at us again? I assume he has called me inside the room because he wants us to be intimate. But Sahil jumps to sit on his bed casually and asks, 'How do you feel?'

'What do you mean?' I ask. *Has he been able to sense the fact that I have remembered something?*

'What?' he throws back at me, 'I mean, how do you feel after meeting my mom? You were so nervous earlier.'

'Oh,' I exclaim, and my body relaxes. 'She's lovely. Friendly. So warm and energetic.'

Sahil smiles at me. He is glad that my perception of his mother is so positive. My mind wanders back to my flashback. I am happy that I have recollected something from my past, but it has left me with a lot of questions. To divert my mind, I look around Sahil's room and see a guitar hanging on the wall.

'Can I play it?' I ask, hoping it will change my mood.

'Do you remember how to?' He raises his eyebrows in surprise. 'You used to love playing it.'

'Did I? I don't remember.' I pick it up from the stand.

I run my fingers on the guitar strings and once I am holding it properly, I play something. A very short melody. I don't know how I know how to play it, but I feel a strange familiarity with the tune.

Sahil gets up from the bed and stops me midway. He has an amazed look on his face and is staring at me with curiosity.

'What happened?' I ask, keeping the guitar on the table I have been leaning against.

'How did you remember how to play that?' he asks. He is looking at me as if he has just witnessed a miracle.

'I don't know how I did it. It just came to me naturally.'

'Nandini ... it's the same song that you used to play for me. For us.'

20

Nandini: Don't Remember Your Past

If one day I have an accident and lose my memory, how will you make me remember you, remember us and our relationship? I read out aloud.

A couple of days after meeting Sahil's mother, we are chilling in a café. I am reading a book and Sahil is busy on his phone.

Sahil looks up at me with a confused look on his face at my words, probably wondering why I am behaving so strangely. From his point of view, I *am* acting strange. But if someone knew what was going on in my mind, they'd understand why I wasn't being my normal self. Even now, two days later, I cannot believe what had happened at Sahil's house. I had been under the impression that I was just a lost soul floating helplessly along with the tides of life. I had thought there was no hope of recovery for me. But Sahil had come into my life like a ray of sunshine. And now after that flashback and the tune that I had somehow managed to recollect, it feels like I am on the cusp of a major discovery.

'Will you tell me please what's on your mind?' Sahil pulls the book away from my hands. 'I am sorry I couldn't come to college yesterday. I had to go out for some work for Dad. That's why I didn't get any time to even talk with you,' he sighs.

I wait for him to finish and then say, 'It's not that. It's not about yesterday. It's about the day before. At your house.'

He struggles to remember what had happened that day. 'I don't understand. Can you please speak clearly?'

I muster up my courage and lean towards him. 'Tell me something. Has your mom ever caught us together while we have been holding hands?'

'What? When?' Sahil is perplexed and he narrows his eyes, trying to recollect. 'Nothing of that sort happened the day before.'

'I am not talking about the day before. I mean, did something like that happen anytime in the past? Sometime when we were at your place, and your mom caught us? I think we had been watching television together when that happened, and I suppose there had been other women in the house, including my mom.' I share a part of the flashback I'd had.

'Wa ... it ... wait.' He stutters in an effort to absorb what I am saying. 'What are you talking about?'

'Please tell me.' I don't repeat myself because I know he has understood what I am talking about.

'Okay,' he sighs. 'Yes, that happened. It happened in the first month of our relationship when our parents hadn't known we had started dating. They had just known that we were friends and my mom had been caught off guard when she had seen us. But we were just holding hands and nothing more,' Sahil tells me, and then asks, 'But why did you ask me that?'

'That means it's happening,' I say. It still hasn't dawned on Sahil that I have actually remembered a memory from the past. I don't know how to react, knowing now that the memory had been real, and not a hallucination.

'What's happening?' He looks at me anxiously. A second later, it clicks and he asks, 'But how did you remember that?'

'I think my memories ... they are coming back.'

He is astonished to hear that. 'Is that the thing troubling you?' he asks.

'Yes,' I answer but I don't sound convincing.

Sahil doesn't buy it either. 'Are you sure? Because it doesn't seem so.'

He is right. I still haven't told him about my father. So much has happened since that day that I am confused about what I remember and what I don't. And now, these old memories have popped up. 'There's another thing I haven't told you,' I say.

'What?' He is looking wary from having received so many shocking revelations.

'It's not just one memory that's back. Someone else has come back too. My father.'

His jaw drops. 'Your father?'

I nod and tell him everything that Maasi shared with me—about my father's visit to Maasi's place, about him wanting me back, about how he belonged to an influential family because of which he had dumped my mom.

'And you are telling me all this now?' A worried look flashes across his face. 'Nandini, promise me you'll stop going to college by bus from now on. Okay? Please, it's too dangerous.' The concern in his eyes touches me.

I try telling him to not worry and that I am capable of handling my father. 'But Megha is always with me. And why would he be dangerous?'

But Sahil is adamant. 'I don't want to hear anything.' He hugs me; his arms feel like a warm blanket on a cold night. His presence is a huge relief. Every time I feel like I am falling apart—unable to handle the emotional turmoil—the only thing that holds me together is his love. As he holds me tight, tears start flowing down my face. Sahil's arms are my safe zone—to cry, relax and to let out all my pain.

He wipes my tears and says, 'And what if you meet him? Will you consider going back with him?'

I smile amidst the tears as I look at his worried face. Sahil thinks I will leave him again. I ruffle his hair playfully, finding his expression endearing. His question tells me how badly he wants me in his life, how much he loves me.

'Of course not. I'll never ever leave you. You are my lifeline. I promise.' I pause and add to myself quietly, 'But one thing is certain. If my father comes to meet me, I will get my answers from him.'

An hour later, we have finished our coffee and fries. Sahil insists on dropping me home, especially now that he knows about my father. He fears that my father is most likely my stalker. It has started raining heavily as we leave.

'Nandini, please don't let all of this affect your studies. Have you caught up with the others?' he asks.

I am about to answer, but before I can, my body suddenly stiffens. This time, instead of an image, I hear a woman's voice, coming from a distance.

Nandini ... close your eyes. Don't worry, nothing will happen to us.

There is a sense of panic in that voice. Her voice keeps getting louder and louder in my head with each passing second and Sahil's voice keeps fading. My eyes scan all around us to see if there is anyone around. But there is no one except Sahil, who has just started noticing that I am panicking.

I can see his lips moving but I can't hear what he is saying. The woman's voice keeps speaking, sending chills down my spine. I want to tell Sahil about what is happening to me, but it seems as if someone has sealed my lips shut.

Nandini ... run, just run.

The woman's voice continues echoing in my ears. Seconds later, I hear the sound of car tyres screeching and I am paralysed. But when I look over at Sahil, he is driving normally. I am safe. But the woman has still not stopped talking and I clamp my hands on my ears to stop the voice. But to no avail. I close my eyes, terrified about what is happening, and hear the sound of a car crashing. The car rolls over twice. I am petrified as I lie on the side of the road, trapped inside the car. The broken shards of glass and metal are cutting into my skin. The weight of the car is pressing down on the lower half of my body with immense force. I cannot move! I can feel the metallic taste of blood in my mouth. I start counting my last breaths, like a fish out of water gasping for air.

The last thing I hear is, *I am sorry, beta. I tried. Forgive me.*

21

Nandini: I Saw Him Again

I wake up to a familiar smell of sanitisers and antiseptics. It doesn't take me long to realise I am in a hospital. *Why am I here again?* I ask myself and suddenly remember the car accident.

'Sahil,' I scream and try to lift myself up into a sitting position out of sheer panic. He is sitting right in front of me on a stool beside the bed.

'I'm here,' he says and rubs my palms to calm my nerves.

His voice soothes me. 'Are you alright?' I ask, trying to look for wounds on his body but I find none.

'I am absolutely fine. But what happened to you?'

'I thought we had an ...' *Had I hallucinated about a car crash?* I realise that must be so since Sahil is sitting in front of me alive and unharmed. There are no bruises or wounds on his body. 'Forget that. What happened with me?' I ask him without revealing any details of the accident.

'You fainted! And scared the hell out of me. I brought you here immediately and have also informed your Maasi. She'll be here any minute,' Sahil says. He gets up and pours some water in a glass. 'Have some water,' he says, handing it over to me. 'The doctor is saying you are absolutely fine. All the tests are normal. So, what happened? Did you have a flashback again?'

'Yes. I heard a woman's voice shouting, and then I saw our car flipping over ...'

Sahil is shocked at the details. Just thinking about the flashback has left my body trembling again. He immediately embraces me and kisses me on the forehead. 'Don't worry, you are fine now,' he tells me.

He makes me lie back on the bed and adjusts the pillow under my head. 'The doctors want to keep you under observation for a day.' He rolls his eyes and adds, 'I wanted to stay over with you tonight but I can't. Only relatives are allowed. Boyfriends have no place in the Indian system of kinship.'

I laugh and tap his wrist with my hand. 'Go and get some sleep. I am fine.'

'I don't want to leave you alone,' he says.

'Trust me, I am fine.' He looks tired and clearly needs some rest.

He caresses my cheek and starts running his fingers through my hair. 'Promise me you won't think about your past. Promise me you won't try to make sense of your flashback and stress yourself out,' he says.

'I won't,' I reassure him.

It is only after several confirmations and promises from me that Sahil finally gives in and agrees to go home once Maasi arrives. He closes the door and waves at me through the small window. I wave back till he vanishes out of my sight. He will probably sit outside the door until Maasi arrives.

When she does, she looks stricken. I realise that the same worry is on her face that I had seen on the day I had woken up from my coma. It is only when I tell her that the doctors say I'll be fine that she calms down a bit.

After having dinner and taking my medicines, I try to sleep but I can't. Despite the heavy antibiotics, my mind keeps wandering back to the morning's flashback.

The voice that I'd heard was probably my Mom's. She was screaming, telling me to close my eyes, reassuring me that nothing would happen to us. Had she not wanted me to see something? Or someone? I remember her asking me to run, but what had she meant by that? Who were we running away from? Why had we been escaping from Khajjiar overnight without telling anyone? I need to find out the reasons. I have to. Maybe the car crash wasn't really an accident. Maybe it had been deliberate. Maybe Mom's death hadn't been an accident at all.

I am sorry, beta, I tried. Her words play in my mind.

By now it is quite late at night, Maasi is in deep sleep on the couch beside me bed. I feel bad for her. After working the whole day in the beauty parlour, she is now having to spend the night on an uncomfortable couch. Not to mention the mental agony that I am clearly putting her through. She has already suffered a lot in the past year and I'm still making life difficult for her.

I turn my gaze towards the door and immediately break out into goosebumps all over my body. I can see a shadow outside. I can also see someone's shoes through the gap between the floor and the bottom of the door. Someone is staring at me through the small window in the door. I am about to wake Maasi up when the shadow disappears. I can even hear the faint footsteps of someone walking away. Someone had been watching me. I wonder if I could be hallucinating again. But it had felt so real. My heart feels heavy with fear.

After that incident, I cannot sleep the whole night. My eyes stay fixed at the door. But the shadow doesn't reappear.

I rest for a day after being discharged, but join college soon after. Sahil picks me up from home to take me to college like he had said he would. Once we reach, we see Megha and Kartik waiting for us in the corridor.

'Nandini!' Megha sees my pale face and says, 'We heard about what happened. Are you okay now?'

'I am better,' I nod.

Kartik correctly assumes that I am still a little weak. 'You should have rested for one more day. You clearly need it.'

'I can't keep lagging behind in my studies. I don't want to waste one more year. And it's just fatigue, nothing else,' I reply, defensively.

'Okay, but take care of yourself,' Kartik says and points at Sahil. 'Because when you aren't there, he chews my brains. You better stay fit so that he can remain busy with you.' Both he and Megha chuckle at his words.

Sahil has been silent all morning and doesn't respond to Kartik's joke either. After Megha and Kartik leave, I smile at him. 'See you in the evening,' I say.

Sahil nods and I leave for my lectures. I can imagine what is going on in his mind. He is worried because my memories are returning. Maybe he is worried about something that had happened between us the last time—something I don't remember and he does. But this is all conjecture. I don't know what had happened. But Sahil's words to me, *'Promise me, you won't think about the past'* bother me for some reason.

Sometimes I feel like I am overthinking all this, but now that I know there is a possibility that Mom and I may have been running away from someone, how can I not? I decide to talk to Sahil to reassure him that I won't disappear again. I am ready to do whatever it takes to let him know that I won't break up with him again.

After the lunch break, an office assistant comes to my class and calls out my name. He says the student representative wants to meet me. I take permission from my professor and leave the class. I wonder what could have happened, why she would want to meet me all of a sudden. She is sitting behind a table and working on some files when she sees me and asks, 'You are Nandini Kashyap, right?' I nod. 'Your father is waiting for you inside.'

What the fuck! He had finally found his way to me!

22

Nandini: Does He Really Love Me?

My father wants to meet me. He's right there inside that room. I have never seen him before. I have no idea what he looks like. Maasi hasn't ever shown me his picture. Maybe she doesn't have one. But how will I know if the person inside the meeting room is really my father or if he is some impersonator? Someone who has been stalking me or hiding behind hospital doors at night? If he really is my father, wouldn't I feel some sort of an attachment towards him when I meet him for the first time? I have wanted to meet him for so long, and that moment has now arrived. This is the time for me to get some answers.

There is a tornado tearing through my mind and heart. Last night I had dreamed about my mother. I had been lying next to her on a hospital bed. I had felt so comforted in her embrace. We hadn't been able to see each other because the room had been dark. She had caressed my face and kissed my forehead. The moment had felt so real. But on some level, I'd known that I was dreaming. I forced myself to wake up. When I finally awoke, I realised I was covered in sweat.

I don't know why I had that dream. But it is possible that it was because thoughts of my father taking me away with him had been troubling me. Ever since Maasi told me that my father was back, I have waited for the day he would come to meet me, with both anticipation and fear. And now that day is here. The man who has known about me all my life is waiting for me on the other side of the door. Why has he come all the way to my college to meet me? But I know the answer to that as soon as the question pops up in my head. Maasi and Uncle will never allow him to enter their house. I hesitate as I place my hand on the door knob.

What if my father decides to take me along with him right now? No, he can't do that. I am an adult. I have the right to choose where I want to go. And I have decided what I want. I'll live here in Kangra. In Maasi's home. With her family. My family. And with Sahil. If my father really wants to be with me, he has to be the one to shift here.

It is time to face him. Mostly because I want answers. I walk inside and see a well-dressed man—black suit, crisp blue shirt neatly tucked in, grey hair, razor sharp nose, a sparsely wrinkled, emotionless face. Our eyes meet and it feels as if time has come to a stop. I watch him walk towards me, the sound of his shoes the only sound in the room. Is this the sound I had heard in the hospital when I'd heard someone walking away from my door? With every step towards me, his smile widens and his face is no longer emotionless.

'You are Nandini,' he says.

I don't answer him. I stand there not feeling the need to respond to his words. I can see the guilt in his eyes for staying away from me for so many years. He inches closer to hold me by my shoulders, but I, instinctively, take a step back. He can see my discomfort, but he still introduces himself. 'I am your father. Harshvardhan Chowdhary.'

My heart starts racing, my palms have become sweaty, and my mind is struggling with all kinds of thoughts. Intrusive thoughts that don't make any sense are racing through my head. 'I don't believe you,' I say sternly, hoping my face doesn't betray my confusion.

He removes a piece of folded paper from his pocket and hands it to me. I see that it is my birth certificate. My name is on it.

Nandini Chowdhary.
Mother's name: Asha Kashyap.
Father's name: Harshvardhan Chowdhary.

I hand it back to him and say in disgust, 'I am not a Chowdhary.'

He doesn't respond and quietly puts the paper back in his pocket. 'It's an old certificate. Your mother must have removed my name from yours when I refused to marry her.'

You deserved that! I scream in my head. The room falls silent again. He can see me avoiding eye contact with him and rubbing my hands in nervousness. 'I am sorry. I know I wasn't there for you when you needed me. Not when Asha passed away. Not when you were in a coma.'

How does he have all this information? And what does he mean? Does he still care about me? I break my silence and say,

'What's the use of telling me all this now? I am sure you aren't here to give me condolences. What do you want?'

I give a heartless laugh after saying this, pretending to not care that he is standing before me—my father who I have been wanting to meet.

He gives me an intense look. 'Can we talk elsewhere? I can explain.' He can probably guess that I am in no mood to entertain him, so he continues, 'Please, if you don't mind.'

'No.' I am adamant and go to sit on the vacant chair next to the desk. 'Tell me whatever you have to right here. I have lectures to attend.'

He sighs. 'I am sorry, Nandini. I know just saying sorry probably isn't enough to make up for all these years I have been absent. And I can't erase all the things I have done in the past. But trust me, I am a changed man now and want a chance to be your father again. I'll probably never be able to compensate for your lost childhood, for not having a father figure in your life. But please give me a chance to mend things,' he pleads. Even I can sense, the grief in his voice. He sounds genuine, but I am still not sure if I can trust him.

'I wasn't able to fulfil my commitments towards you and your mother, when I was dating her in Delhi. I had promised to talk to my parents about her so that we could get married. But then she got pregnant with you and somehow, before I could tell my parents about us, they came to know everything. Asha had just newly joined our company as a secretary to my father. Once my relationship with her was out in the open, he made sure that she left the city and broke all ties with our family. At that time, I neither had the courage to stop him nor the confidence to go along with her. I know I left her completely alone when she needed me the most.'

'So, you do nothing for nineteen years and now after so much time has passed, you come here to mend bridges with your so-called daughter?' I ask, wanting to know if he really cared about me as he was saying or if he had some ulterior motive like Maasi believed.

My question takes him by surprise. His guilt-ridden face doesn't change. 'I had no idea where your mother went after she left Delhi. I tried looking for you both so many times after that, but I was never successful.'

'You're making up stories!'

'No, I am not. Trust me. I don't know what Usha has told you. But I genuinely want you to come to Delhi and live with me. My parents are no more. You are all I have in this world. Will you please come with me?'

Before I'd met him, I had been firm that I wouldn't give him another chance, but now, if I am being honest with myself, his words have melted my resolve a little. I get the feeling that he truly wants to make amends. A part of me is regretting that I was so heartless with him earlier.

Nandini, you are being too harsh on him. At least hear him out. What if he really has changed? What if his feelings towards you are genuine? You never got to experience a father's love and now that your mother is no longer in this world, and your father wants to mend things with you, shouldn't you at least give him one chance? Even if you decide to not go to Delhi with him, the least you can do is spend some time with him here. Give yourself some time to get to know him, his world and whether you can really be a part of it. Nandini, he is your only living parent. You should at least make an effort to believe him.

Another part of me is furious with the story he is telling me about how all those years ago he hadn't had the courage to stand up to his parents so that he could have been with me and my mother.

Nandini, don't believe anything he says. He is the same man who once abandoned your mom. Like a coward he backed out from his biggest commitment right when you were about to be born. He has never been there when you have needed him. And now he is back to shatter the fragile normalcy that you have achieved in the last few months. What if he abandons you again? All those years ago he had robbed your mother of all her happiness and now he is here, asking you to forgive him for everything that he put her through. And what about Sahil? You promised him that you would never leave him again. How can you abandon Sahil when he loves you so much? Wouldn't it be exactly like what your father did to your mother? Promise the world and then walk away without a second thought?

I am so confused that there is only one thing left to do: leave his presence immediately. 'Do one thing,' I say as I stand up from the chair, 'just leave me alone.' I turn around to leave when he stops me, 'Nandini ... please wait.'

I look back at him. He hands over a business card to me and says, 'My personal number is mentioned here. Anytime you feel like talking to your father, please call me.'

I take the card and leave without saying another word.

23

Nandini: United in Love!

My last class gets cancelled and I go in search of Sahil and Kartik's lecture room on the second floor. I couldn't concentrate on any of my lectures today after my father's visit. I am still unsure about whether I should tell Maasi about it. That information would surely worry both her and my uncle. And Sahil? If he came to know that I had met my father, he would probably not leave me alone even for a second. He is anyway so fearful that I would disappear from his life again.

By the time, I reach their classroom, I still have no clarity on what I should do about my father's visit, but I put it out of my mind for the time being. I can overhear Sahil and Kartik deep in conversation ; probably their lecture was cancelled too.

Just as I'm about to greet them, I hear Sahil saying, 'You are out of your mind.'

'I am serious, dude. These mini photo copies of the answer sheets can save both of us in the exams. Trust me.'

They are clearly discussing about cheating in the upcoming internal examination.

'Have you lost it, Kartik? We'll both be badly fucked if someone comes to know about this and if we get caught,' Sahil says angrily, standing up from his chair.

'Bro, believe me, no one will come to know. Exams are just a week away and we haven't even started studying yet. How will we complete the entire syllabus in such a short time?'

'I know what you are saying, but this isn't the solution to the problem,' Sahil replies firmly.

They are sitting in an empty classroom and are still not aware of my presence. I enter the room from the back door.

'What are you guys up to?' I ask.

Both of them turn around to look at me in shock. Sahil quickly runs up to me and gives me a hug. 'Hey, when did you come in?' he asks with a smile.

'Come, sit down,' Kartik suggests, pointing to the bench in front of them. 'We were just discussing the upcoming exams. I think it's time to get serious about studies.'

'I know how serious you are!' I say sarcastically and Kartik's smile turns into a frown. 'Are you really thinking of cheating in the exam?'

Kartik's face falls, but he composes himself quickly and says, 'Oh God, it's not what you think. I was just joking.' His eyes dart towards Sahil.

'There's no need to cheat in the exam. Got it, guys?' I say in a commanding tone.

'Okay, my lord! As you say,' Sahil says teasingly and both he and Kartik execute a mock bow in front of me.

I grin at their tomfoolery. 'Stop mocking me. Let's leave now.' We move out of the classroom. 'By the way, where's Megha?' I ask.

'She's gone to submit her assignment,' Kartik replies. He takes out his phone from his pocket to call her. 'Okay ... okay, we'll wait for you at the gate,' he says into the phone.

Once we reach the gate, I see Rudra approaching us. *What does he want now?* I think to myself. But he isn't here to talk to me. Instead, he wants to have a conversation with Sahil. That comes as a surprise! After the lounge incident, I had expected them to never want to see each other's faces again. Sahil isn't very pleased to see him. Rudra, however, looks anxious and terrified.

'Sahil, please listen to me. Just once,' he says as soon as he is close enough.

But Sahil pushes Rudra away, shouting, 'I told you to never come near me again.'

Rudra doesn't give up, nor does he retaliate. His voice continues to be soft. 'I am sorry,' he says and steals a glance at me. I can see he is really worried. He looks back at Sahil and says, 'Please don't damage my career.'

My eyes widen in confusion. *What is happening?* 'Why did he say that? How can you damage his career?' I ask Sahil.

I look at everyone, including Kartik, to understand what is really happening and why I'm being kept in the dark about it. When no one responds, I turn to ask Rudra but Sahil stops me. 'Nandini, please stay out of this.' To Rudra he says tersely, 'And you, I can't do anything. Just leave.'

Rudra continues to plead with Sahil. 'Please. I was supposed to submit my thesis in a week. But now the professor says he won't accept it. Don't do that to me. Please.'

'Can someone tell me what is happening?' I say, looking at all of them.

There's a moment of silence and then Rudra speaks up. 'Sahil's dad is a trustee of this college. And a politician of the ruling party.' My jaw drops on hearing this. I had absolutely no idea that Sahil's father was the trustee of our college. 'Nandini, please tell him. I would have never done what I did with you if I hadn't been high on drugs. I never meant to insult you. Please!'

Sahil ignores Rudra and we all start walking away from him. Megha reaches us at the same time. She stares at Rudra in annoyance and says, 'Why is he here?'

'To beg in front of Sahil,' Kartik replies.

He reveals nothing more, but Megha chuckles as if she is already aware of the whole matter. *Am I the only one who is in the dark about this? Sahil had told me that his dad was a businessman. But was he also a part of the college management? Is this why Kartik was so confident about cheating, knowing that Sahil would bail them out using his father's influence?* All this is starting to sound very unethical.

I grip my fingers tightly around Sahil's arm in anger and ask him, 'Is it right to take advantage of your dad's position so that you can drag someone down?'

'Nandini, I haven't done anything.' He tries to sound genuine, but I have a strong feeling that he is lying to me.

'But if that's the case, why did Rudra come to you for help?' I want more answers.

'I don't know.' He walks on brushing off my question.

Kartik and Megha are listening silently without interfering. But I want to know why he hasn't told me about his father and his connections earlier.

'Why didn't you tell me that your dad's a college trustee?'

This time he stops and looks at me. 'Would that have changed anything?'

'No ... but ...' I am at a loss for words. Sahil isn't wrong to question me because it hardly matters who his father is. But before I can say anything more, he ends the conversation. 'Great. Then let's not talk about Rudra anymore.'

'Agreed!' Megha says finally. 'Sometimes it's better to let go of things. Probably that's the best way to remain happy and have a healthy relationship. Let's go and have a good time together. From tomorrow, it's only studies for all of us. I don't want to waste this evening.'

I, too, brush off my concerns about Rudra. Sahil is right; as usual I am overthinking things.

Kartik decides that we should drive up to the top of one of the Kangra hills in Sahil's car. A turquoise coloured stream winds its way along the road as we drive on. Babbling and burbling, it springs over the limestone rocks in the way, whisking pebbles along that look like floating pieces of glitter. When we reach the top, I am awed by the size and majesty of the trees around us. Their knotted branches rise upwards in the sky for as far as the eye can see. The chirping of birds is like a soft, melodious orchestra for our ears. The pleasant wind carries the mulchy fragrance of the forest. I feel joyous to be here.

'I never knew that Kangra was so beautiful,' I exclaim, inhaling the fresh air.

'But it's not as beautiful as you,' Sahil says hugging me.

I look down shyly. Kartik and Megha are close by. Kartik doesn't miss the opportunity to pull my leg. 'You guys can kiss each other. We won't mind.' He winks at Megha. 'Isn't it, Megha?'

'Yes, you can even go beyond that,' Megha joins in with a chuckle.

'Shut up, guys.' I laugh along with the others.

'Okay listen ... listen, I have something for Megha,' Kartik says and takes out a letter from his pocket. He goes down on his knee and says, 'I love you, Megha. This is not just a letter; the words in this are the true feelings of my heart.'

Sahil puts his arms around me and pulls me closer as we watch the two lovebirds.

'That's too filmy, Kartik,' Sahil teases.

I punch him in the arm and say, 'Girls love these kinds of things. Not everyone falls in love with an angry young man like you.'

'Do I look like an angry young man to you?'

'Ask anyone. They would all agree with me.'

He laughs and ruffles my hair, as I silently pout. Megha is quietly reading the letter and blushing away, when Sahil snatches the letter from her hand. Megha does her best to take it back but Sahil has already started reading the letter aloud

'I've always been someone who finds it difficult to put his feelings into words. But today I have dared to write my feelings down. I promise you that I will always do my best to make you feel loved. For me, you are the most beautiful girl in the world. I have seen you feeling low in the past because of your inability to run. But please don't feel that way. Steadiness and stability are more important in life and you ...'

Before Sahil can read any further, Kartik manages to snatch the letter back from him. We all grin at each other. To be honest, in the last few days, I have loved making new memories with these guys rather than trying to remember my past ones.

'It's raining,' Megha says as she leans her head out of the backseat window of the car, on our way home. 'Nandini, do what I'm doing,' she says, swirling her hand outside the window trying to emulate waves.

As I start to do the same thing, dark clouds start to thunder loudly. It sounds like the roar of a monster and I quickly sit back in my seat. Sahil continues to drive, not noticing how my hands are holding the seat belt in a tight grip. I see lightning flash across the dark sky and my heart starts beating violently. I know what is going to come next. This feeling is eerily like déjà vu. Suddenly, a memory flashes in front me.

There's a blurry figure of a man who has broken into our house. He has a violent argument with my mom and then he attacks her. Instinctively, I pick some heavy object lying close by and hit him hard on the head. He falls to the floor. I rush to see if Mom is okay, but the man quickly gets up from where he has been lying and starts pulling at my legs. I trip, hitting my face on the ground. My nose starts bleeding. Then I hear him say, 'Now, I'll make her suffer.'

Mom is also lying on the floor close by. Her eyes half shut she says, 'Nandini ... run, just run.'

I gather all my strength to get up, only to be pushed back onto the sofa by the man. He jumps on top of me and tries to force himself on me. He tears off most of my clothes in the process. I try to push him away but he is too strong for me. From the corner of my eye, I can see Mom struggling to get up. Somehow, she manages to do that, coming closer to hit the man with the same heavy object I had used. This time he collapses on the floor, unconscious. Mom and I start to run out of the house. We reach our car, quickly getting in. Mom starts to race away from our house. I look down to see bruises all over my body; even mom is bleeding. But we are okay because we have escaped that awful man. I can't stop crying as Mom says, 'Nandini ... close your eyes. Don't worry, nothing will happen to us.'

But just a few seconds later, I hear the sound of car tyres screeching, followed by a loud crash. Our car rolls over twice on the road, trapping my mom and me inside. The broken shards of glass and metal are cutting into my skin painfully. The weight of the car is pressing down on the lower half of my body with immense force. I cannot move! I can feel the metallic taste of blood in my mouth. I start counting my last breaths, like a fish out of water gasping for air.

'I am sorry, beta. I tried. Forgive me.'

I hear those words again and again, and it soon gets unbearable. I yell, 'Sahil, stop the car!'

At hearing my cry, everyone in the car almost jumps out of their seats. Sahil speaks first. 'What happened, Nandini? Shit, you are sweating.'

Kartik and Megha also lean forward in their seat to calm me down. He is blabbering something and Megha is patting my back. But none of this registers in my mind. 'Sahil ... stop the car, please.'

He panics looking at me. 'Okay, okay, give me a moment.'

As soon as he stops the car, I rush outside and start gasping for air. My eyes feel so heavy that I have to close them. But when I open them, I see myself lying on the side of the road with my dying mom right next to me.

24

Nandini: I Want to Die

I stand at the edge of the road holding my spinning head. I don't know how to stop the spinning. Sahil steps out of the car. He immediately gets drenched in the pouring rain. From the corner of my eye, I can also see Megha and Kartik rushing towards me with an umbrella. I hold up my hand to stop them from coming near me. The others stop, but Sahil ignores my request and takes a step closer to me. I take a step back and hold up my hand again, asking him to stay away. He finally understands that I need space right now. I am grateful for that.

Images keep flashing in front of my eyes as if a slideshow is playing in front of me. I force my eyes shut, unable to bear the images. But the moment I shut my eyes, my memories take over. Me—an eight-year-old—with Maasi and Mom at the Bajreshwari temple. Me—a teenager, probably 14 years old—with Mom at some overnight camp. Me—from a few years back—having dinner with Mom and Sahil's mother. Me and my mom, at our old house, which is not as big as Sahil's or even Maasi's, but is cute and rustic. Sahil and I, in a movie theatre, holding hands. Sahil and I, at his home, cuddling on the sofa while his mom is in the kitchen. Uncle, giving Rashi and me gifts along with a daughter's day card. Maasi, Uncle, Rashi and I, on a long drive, up a hill. Rashi and I playing together, happy to be together, sharing secrets with each other.

I am not hallucinating. These are all my memories, images from my life. Memories I have been trying to recall for such a long time, and now I have. But with these memories come the questions, for which I have no answers. The memories are like the unsolved pieces of the puzzle of my life. Mom's words come back to me.

'I am sorry, beta. I tried. Forgive me.'

The flashes finally stop. But I realise, my life has completely changed in a matter of minutes. I now have some idea of what had happened with me and my mother on the night of the accident.

'Nandini, you are scaring me,' Sahil interrupts my train of thought. 'Are you okay?'

I nod and Sahil helps me get back into the car. He starts driving and I notice that his clothes are soaked just like mine. 'Sorry, Sahil. But you know what I am going through. I hope you understand.'

'Don't be sorry,' he says gently. He runs his fingers through my hair. 'Did you have flashes of any more memories?' he asks.

'Yes. Quite a lot of them,' I answer.

I haven't yet told Megha about my flashbacks, so she is rightly shocked. 'Oh God, you are recollecting your past? Seriously? That's amazing.'

I nod. But how do I tell her that there is nothing amazing about it? I feel like I'm losing myself as the past is pulling me towards it. I am completely shaken by the few memories I have managed to remember. Every memory has only left me with more questions, and has further complicated my life.

'Do you need some water?' Kartik asks.

I take the bottle from him and gulp the water down as fast as I can to calm myself. But nothing is working.

'Let's go home,' Sahil suggests.

'No,' I blurt out. I don't want to go home. There is another place I need to go to. 'I want to go somewhere else. Please.'

'Okay, where?'

I tell Sahil about my destination and he stares at me blankly. But thankfully, he doesn't ask me any more questions, and starts driving again. My mind is in turmoil and the visuals of the past keep coming back to me. Soon, we arrive at our destination—the Bajreshwari temple. It is still raining heavily but that doesn't stop me from stepping out of the car. I turn around and tell all of them, 'Wait in the car. I'll be back soon.' Megha agrees and shouts, 'Nandini, please be careful. At least take an umbrella.'

But Sahil is adamant. 'I am coming along with you. I can't leave you alone in this condition.' He looks extremely worried, 'Look at you—you're shivering.'

'Please, I'll manage,' I tell him and start walking towards the temple gate.

There is a mad rush of something—maybe excitement—roaring through my veins. I know this place holds some of the answers I most need. I reach the place where I had felt my mom's presence the last time. I stand there and close my eyes, willing her to come to me again. A few minutes go by, but I feel nothing. There is no unnatural force around me like the last time. I look around, hoping to somehow see some sort of a vision of her. But I am all alone. Is this happening because my mind isn't at peace? I close my eyes again. This time, I see the blurred figure of a man trying to overpower me—the image I had seen earlier—and I instantly open my eyes again. I touch my mother's name etched on the marble stone and can't control myself anymore. Thankfully, the rain hides my tears and allows me to grieve my mother's loss in peace. I drop down to my knees in front of the marble.

Mom, I wish you were here to console me about what had happened that night. All this while, I had wanted to know the truth about that night. And now that I do, I am shattered. I want to die. Why didn't you take me along with you that night, that night when you left me all alone? The reality of what happened that night has scared me out of my wits. I don't know who to believe, who to trust. And what about Sahil? Do I tell him about the memories that have just resurfaced? Then there's Dad too. He wants me to go with him to Delhi. I have no answers, I feel so lost.

I don't know how long I have been kneeling there crying to myself. I only stop when I hear Sahil's voice. He runs towards me and hugs me tightly.

'What's happening to you, Nandini? Please you have to trust me. You have to tell me what's going on,' he cries. 'I know you are hiding something from me. When you keep things to yourself, I feel so helpless—as if I mean nothing to you. Please tell me. What has happened? What was the flashback like this time?'

Sahil gently rubs my back to soothe me and to stop me from trembling. I embrace him tightly. I'm scared I might lose him if I tell him the truth. So I grip him tighter, never wanting to let him go.

I miss you, Mom.

Memories—they can either make you or break you. Mine are definitely breaking me apart. Sahil guides me back to the car, and we drive away from the temple. After dropping Kartik and Megha home, he parks the car at a spot near his house which overlooks the valley. We get out of the car and silently go, sit on a nearby rock from where we have the full, glorious view of the valley. We stay silent for a while, not exchanging a word, just staring at the setting sun. Once Sahil is sure that I've had enough time to settle down and regain my composure, he says, 'Now will you tell me what has happened? I want to know but only if you want to tell me.'

'Sahil, I never want to hide anything from you.' I glance at him.

He picks up a stone and flings it into the abyss in front of us. He does it again. He keeps picking up stones and flinging them in the valley. I know what he is doing. He isn't just throwing stones; he is trying to get rid of his frustration. I'm sure he is worrying about the future of our relationship. I can't blame him because I am the one keeping secrets. 'Then come on, tell me,' Sahil asks again with a hint of desperation in his voice.

I take a deep breath and tell him everything that has happened in the last few days. How my father came to the college and asked me to live with him in Delhi. How some part of me wants to give him another chance. I even tell him about the man whose shadow I'd seen outside my hospital door, though I'm not sure Sahil believes me when I say that. I tell him about my memories of the accident, though I omit to tell him that someone had tried to rape me right before the accident. I don't have the courage to tell him because I have, myself, barely accepted that something so horrible happened to me. I always get the feeling when I'm around Sahil that something bad has happened between Sahil and me in the past. But whatever that maybe, this is much worse. The memory of that horrific violation has left me feeling angry and even empty, as if a part of me died the moment that memory flashed.

'Don't you think you should have told me all this earlier?' Sahil asks me, holding my face in his hand gently.

'Even if I had told you earlier, how could you have helped me? I have to face this alone.' A tear runs down my cheek and onto his fingers.

'You're wrong. You don't need to face anything alone,' Sahil says, wiping away my tears. 'When you don't tell me things, I get worried. It makes me feel like you don't trust me.'

'I trust you. Believe me when I say that. You ...' I falter, '... you told me to not think about the past. I thought you would get angry if I told you about all these memories,' I tell him.

For a moment, I wonder if Sahil knows something about the rape attempt and is trying to hide it from me. Could that be the reason he told me not to think about the past? I know there's something that went wrong between Sahil and me because of which he doesn't want me rooting through my past. But what if he has always known what happened that night and deliberately hid it from me? But Sahil told me that we had broken up before I had disappeared. He also hadn't known anything about my accident.

So, then, how could he have known of that heinous incident? My mind is racing furiously with all these confusing thoughts.

Sahil breaks the silence. 'You have taken my words the wrong way. I only said that because I didn't want you to feel stressed out. I had meant to say that you should start afresh.'

'Start afresh?' I narrow my eyes at him. 'Then what about you? You, too, are connected to my past, right?'

'I know I am and I'll always be with you.' He sighs and says, 'Nandini, you can trust me. A relationship needs trust. If you don't believe in me, in my love for you, things are going to be very difficult for us.'

'I know that.'

I can see the pain in his eyes. I hug him immediately and say, 'I love you, Sahil. Please don't ever leave me. No matter what happens.'

'Never.' Sahil kisses me.

My memories have given me so much pain and now because of them, I have caused pain to Sahil as well. I wish my memories had never returned.

25

Nandini: Finally, We Met

I am in my bedroom alone, looking out of the window and thinking about everything that has happened in the last few days. I haven't slept much in this time. Whenever I lie down on the bed to catch some sleep, I get terrible nightmares and wake up in a sweat. The constant overthinking has given me a headache, but the pills aren't helping. The doctors say I am fine, but I know I am not fine. I feel like I have become a slave to my memories. When they come calling for me, I feel like running away from them out of fear. But when I don't get the answers I want, I start hunting for my memories again.

I still haven't talked to Maasi about my father coming to my college to meet me. I know if I tell her about it, she won't be very happy. She will get even more upset if I tell her that I'm thinking of meeting him again. But I really want to see him once more. I take out his business card from my bag and just stare at it for a while. The thought of calling him has popped in my head more than once, but I am scared to act on it because no one seems to like my father or want him to be around me. I, finally, decide to listen to my heart and pick up the phone to call his number.

When he picks up, I can sense the happiness in my father's voice, especially when I inform him that I am ready to meet him tomorrow.

'Sure. I will pick you up. We can then go to my hotel.' He pauses, and taking a deep breath, says, 'Thank you, beta. I am really happy that you have decided to meet me.'

He probably wants to meet at the hotel because he thinks any other place would be too public for such a meeting. I, instead, ask him to meet me at a restaurant located a few kilometres away from my college. Surprisingly, he agrees. I add, 'Okay then. But don't pick me up. I'll come on my own. I don't want anyone to know that I am bunking college to meet you.'

'As you say. I'll be waiting. Good night.' He disconnects the call.

I stay up for a long time thinking about my father and our meeting tomorrow.

What should I talk to him about? How should I behave? I feel anxious because this will be our first proper meeting. Am I nervous to meet him because he is my biological father or because only he has the answers to all my questions?

The next day, I call Megha and Sahil and tell them both that I'll come to college only after lunch. They find nothing odd in that.

I leave home, with all my thoughts weighing heavily on my mind as usual. I hail a cab and soon reach the place where we had decided to meet. As I'm getting out of the cab, I spot a few bodyguards at the entrance. This freaks me out.

Is he meeting his daughter or some business rival?

I try to keep my nervousness in check as I enter the restaurant. My father stands up to greet me. 'Welcome, and thank you, Nandini,' he says with a smile.

I smile back and ask him about the guards. 'Were they really needed today?'

'I tried to avoid bringing them, but it isn't in my hands. There is a protocol I have to follow,' he replies.

We take our seats. I rest my hands on the table with my fists closed tightly in apprehension. He can see the uneasiness in my body language and says, 'Please feel comfortable.' The calmness in his voice makes me wonder if I'm the only one here who is feeling edgy. After all, he too was meeting me properly for the first time. 'Do you want to order something?' he asks, handing me the menu.

'Just coffee.'

He orders two cups of coffee and then, comes directly to the point. 'Nandini, I really want you to come and live with me in Delhi. We can start afresh and make up for all the time we have lost.'

I stare at him without a word. Maasi had called him the devil incarnate, but I can't see any of that in him. He seems pleased to see me and appears to genuinely want me to live with him. Still, I ignore what he has just said and ask him the question that has been troubling me the most. 'Did you really love my mom? Do you even remember what she looked like?'

The surprised look on his face shows that he isn't expecting this question from me. With a sigh, he says, 'I know you don't believe me. And I also don't know what your Maasi has told you about me. But trust me, I really loved your mother. We were madly in love. But things didn't work out as we had wanted them to. I couldn't go against my parents then. I succumbed to their pressure.'

Should I feel sorry for him or be angry with him for shying away from his responsibilities? Moreover, I have no idea if he is even telling me the truth or just making up a story. But the more he reveals about himself, the more I feel that he isn't as bad as Maasi has portrayed him to be. But why would Maasi lie to me? I keep my thoughts aside and say, 'So you must have married someone else by now and must live with your kids. Where will I fit in your life?'

Before he can answer, the waiter comes to serve the coffee. After he leaves, my father calmly sips his coffee and says, 'No, beta, I never married. I never fell in love again.'

This is not what I was expecting to hear. *He never got married? Had he really loved Mom so much? And does this mean I am his only family which is why he wants me to be a part of his life now?*

I can't hold myself back and ask, 'So if you loved Mom so much, why didn't you stand up for her? Were you so afraid of your parents that you thought it was better to leave my Mom alone when she was pregnant? Why is it that you couldn't even fight for your love then? And now you want to be with me. Why?'

He shifts his gaze away from me. With a heavy voice, he says, 'I can never forgive myself for not standing by Asha. It must not have been easy for her. I acted like a coward then and I am sorry for that.' His guilt-ridden eyes moisten as he continues, 'I tried really hard to find her afterwards but after a point I just lost hope. I know I am to be blamed for not standing up to my family, but I was helpless then.' He pauses and holds my hand. 'I know it's too late to be sorry, but now that I have met you, I don't want to repeat the mistake I made 20 years ago. If we stay together, then at least I can hope for Asha's forgiveness,' he says as he wipes his eyes.

Even though I don't know my father at all, I feel as if I can believe the man in front of me. After all, the past cannot be changed. But he is here now wanting to mend things with me and there is nothing wrong in that. Every word he has said has showed how desperately he wants me in his life. This is a new experience for me. Although Maasi and Uncle both love me, it is the love that my father is showering on me that is making me feel truly special. However, I am still not sure about going to live with him in Delhi. I am not prepared to take such a life-altering decision in haste. And I tell him that.

'Maasi doesn't want me to go with you. And she has been the only one who has been with me and taken care of me since the accident. I need some time to sort out a few things before I make any big decision.'

He happily agrees, 'I have waited for you for so many years that a few more days don't matter.'

We drink our coffees and chat casually for some time. The more I talk to him, the more I feel attached to him. I don't realise when my nervousness vanishes and I become comfortable around my father. When we are about to leave, I express my thoughts openly. 'Thank you. I've had some misconceptions about you all this while. If I hadn't met you today, they would have stayed with me forever.'

'I am always with you whenever you need me,' he says and hugs me.

I don't want him to drop me back to my college so he leaves after saying bye. This has been such a lovely morning and I am glad I decided to meet my father. But the fact that Maasi dislikes him so much doesn't sit right with me. I wish I really knew what had happened to make Maasi feel that way about him.

26

Nandini: Unspoken Feelings

It's been a few days since I met my father at the coffee shop. Exams are just around the corner and I am drowning in my studies. My constant internal struggle is also not helping matters. I am trying to study when I hear Rashi shouting, her voice coming from the living room. Maasi must have thought I have slept, and locked my door to not disturb me. But listening to the commotion outside, I walk up to the door and pin my ear to it.

'You think I party during the weekends and skip classes on weekdays. Right?' I hear Rashi scream.

'What is this behaviour?' Maasi reacts in a loud voice. 'Kapoor aunty and I were just talking casually. You can't tolerate Nandini being praised by anyone. You're jealous of your own sister. Why?'

'Because no one wants to talk about me at home,' Rashi responds immediately as if she was expecting Maasi's question. I knew that Kapoor aunty had visited Maasi earlier today, but not that Rashi was at home at the time. 'You and Papa only care about Nandini. But what about your own daughter? Have you ever asked me what I want, what I need?'

The room becomes quiet for a brief moment. I am hoping no one opens the door to my room and finds me eavesdropping.

'Look, we have discussed this many times.' Maasi says in a calmer voice. 'It's not like that.'

'It *is* like that,' Rashi insists. 'And if you can't see it, then you are lying to yourself or you are blinded by your love for her. You are constantly worried about her—what she likes, what she wants, her mood swings, her health, blah blah. She is allowed to do whatever she wants. No one ever questions her.' Rashi pauses to catch her breath and then continues, 'Even that day, when she was caught with Sahil, no one questioned her. Instead, you told me to keep quiet.'

'I really don't know what you are talking about,' Maasi says. Her volume is lowering with each passing sentence, as if she is slowly losing the will to fight with Rashi.

'I'll tell you, Mom.' Rashi is having an outburst—a huge one—probably from suppressing her feelings for me for such a long time. 'You have forgotten that I am your daughter. You have also forgotten how her mother and Papa tried to destroy both our families. How could you have forgotten all this?'

'Don't bring that up again, Rashi.'

'Okay, fine. I can accept that you like Nandini more than you like me. But at least don't be so blatant about it. It makes me feel worthless. I feel like running away from this house.'

'It's not like that, Rashi.' It seems that Maasi doesn't know what else to say.

'It is like that. You know everything about her. You would personally drop her to college earlier, you give her lunch every day, you know what she likes and doesn't. Have you ever tried to find out what I like? No, right?'

'Why didn't you tell me you felt this way before?' Maasi says, sounding defeated. 'You should have expressed your feelings to me earlier.'

Rashi cries out, 'Why do you think I prefer not expressing my feelings to you? Because I know you will never try to understand them.'

A brief silence follows. I can't see Rashi's expressions, but I can feel the pain in her words. I never realised she was hiding so much torment inside her. It wasn't just about Sahil preferring me over her or my mom's alleged affair with her father. It was also about the validation she sought from her parents. For the first time ever, I feel some sympathy for her. She isn't the reckless or vile girl she always portrays herself to be. I am completely surprised to hear her true feelings. To be honest, I have never given her an opportunity to fully express herself and, I reckon, neither has Maasi.

'I am sorry, beta,' Maasi says, sounding emotional. 'We didn't do it intentionally. But I am sorry if we made you feel this way. We made a mistake. It won't ever happen again.'

I can hear them both crying. After a couples of seconds, Rashi apologises, 'Sorry, Mom.'

Nobody loves an exam day. I don't either. Not because I am not prepared for it but because I have no recollection of ever having sat for an exam, so I don't really know what the experience is going to be like. With all that is happening in my personal life, I haven't been able to study the entire syllabus but I hope I have studied enough to score passing marks. I am anxious and it shows on my face. I don't interact with anyone that morning and quietly enter the examination hall. A bell rings and we are told to keep our bags outside. I am sweating profusely and I keep rubbing my palms to calm myself down. Along with the first-year students, there are some second-year students too who are appearing for the paper again. I find Rashi has been assigned to sit next to me on the same bench in the hall.

I try to forget that she is sitting beside me and concentrate on what I have to do in the next few hours that lie ahead. The question papers are distributed and I feel at ease once I have skimmed through the questions. I know most of the answers and I start writing immediately. It is a three-hour examination. I don't realise when the first hour passes by. I ask for a supplementary sheet and look around only to see everyone engrossed in writing. A few students are exchanging covert looks with each other probably hoping for some answers. I turn towards Rashi and see that she is secretly copying answers from a photocopied paper hidden under her answer sheet. I suddenly remember overhearing Kartik talking about using photocopies to pass the exams. Rashi glances at me for just a second and gives me a look that says I should mind my own business. She continues copying her answers. I decide to ignore her and instead, focus on my exam.

I am halfway through the paper when I notice that a new invigilator has entered the hall for a surprise visit to make sure students are not cheating. I instantly look in Rashi's direction. She has noticed the invigilator too and is looking petrified.

She probably knows that she might get caught and that the consequences of that would be severe.

Suddenly, something occurs to me and I am surprised at myself for having thought of it all. My eyes are still fixed on Rashi who doesn't look up from her answer sheet. Instead, she crumples the photocopy and throws it away. It lands next to my feet. If I hadn't been looking at her throughout, I would have thought that she threw it near me on purpose. But she hadn't, and that wasn't even important anymore. I start thinking furiously, *What am I supposed to do now?*

I try to kick the paper away from me, but luck isn't in my favour. I freeze with terror as I realise that the invigilator has seen me and is now approaching me. In no time, he is standing in front of me.

'Get up from your seat,' he almost shouts at me while picking up the paper from the floor.

I roll my eyes and sigh, 'I can explain.'

He is looking at the crumpled paper while I look at Rashi from the corner of my eye. She is looking dejected, probably guessing what I would do next. She knows that I had seen her cheating and I can get her caught.

'So you were cheating in the examination,' the invigilator looks up at me and says, after scanning the photocopy. 'I saw you kicking this piece of paper away. Don't you dare lie to me!'

'I'm not going to lie, sir,' I say looking down.

'So, you were cheating, right?'

I give Rashi, who is pretending to write in her answer sheet, another look. Then, I look back at the invigilator and say, 'Yes, sir, I was. I am sorry.'

27

Nandini: I'll Fight My Demons!

I have accepted the blame for something I didn't do. I haven't done that because I sympathise with Rashi. It's also not because I think this may be the last straw for Maasi and Uncle as far as Rashi's behaviour is concerned. It is only because Megha's words from the other day still resonate with me. *Sometimes it's better to let go of things. Probably that's the best way to remain happy and have a healthy relationship.* Rashi thanks me after the exam. I can see the guilt in her eyes, but also some gratitude. I want to believe that this incident can become the start of a healthy relationship between us.

Sahil interrupts my thoughts when he asks, 'What were you saying a few days back? About cheating?' He is definitely mocking me.

'Yes, I remember someone talking about morals.' Kartik joins in the party too.

I try my best to control my laughter but eventually give in and we all laugh aloud. In spite of my asking him not to, after the exam, Sahil spoke to his dad who has requested the college management on my behalf to not take strict action against me. I haven't told anyone that Rashi was the one who was actually cheating because, knowing Sahil, he would want to confront her and that's something I want to avoid at all costs. For me, this incident is not about right or wrong; some things are beyond logical explanations.

That day when I reach home, Rashi isn't around but I find Maasi pacing the living room. When she sees me, she widens her eyes in disbelief and says, 'What was the need to do that?'

Though I am aware of what she is referring to, I feign ignorance. 'What are you talking about?'

'Don't act innocent. I got a call from the college office. You were caught copying today,' she says.

So the management hadn't really been that lenient. They had just allowed me to submit my paper in spite of the cheating.

'We'll talk about it later.' I sit on the sofa, deciding it's time to finally tell her about everything that has been going on for the past few days. 'Right now, I want to talk with you.'

'Regarding?' she asks, curiously.

'You knew everything from day one, right?' I ask.

She sits beside me and looks into my eyes, 'What are you talking about?'

Now she is trying to act innocent.

'Maasi, I had told you my memories are returning. So why did you hide the details about that night from me? Why didn't you tell me that Mom and I had been attacked? I was ... that person ...' I choke on the words and start crying.

Maasi comes closer and wraps her arms around me. She lets me cry it out and I do just that, burying my face in her arms like a kid. I repeat my question and she apologises. 'I am sorry I didn't tell you earlier. But I did not intend to hurt you.' She sighs, gets up from the sofa and walks across the room to sit at the dining table. 'You had just recovered from a tragic incident. You were starting a new life. The doctors had agreed with my decision to not tell you anything as they feared the ensuing shock could be risky for you.'

She pours herself some water from a bottle kept on the dining table and slowly sips from her glass. I wait patiently for her to say more. I have stopped crying by now, but my heart is still in a turmoil. Maasi continues, 'I care for you. I don't know if this is the right thing to say, but I'm glad you suffered from memory loss after the accident. That way I could avoid telling you the horrible truth. Moreover, we weren't sure if your memories would ever return. It didn't make sense telling you something that you may have never remembered yourself.'

'Didn't you inform the police about the attack on us after the doctors informed you of what had happened?' I ask, painfully.

'I did. I used to go to the police station every day initially, but they found no proof of any attack. There were no CCTV cameras around the house which we could have used. Finally, the police just closed the case. You don't know how heartbreaking it was for me to know what Asha and you went through, and still not be able to do anything about it. I hope you understand that there was nothing more I could do.'

I nod my head. I finally understand why she has always been so protective towards me. It was her fear for me mixed with the love she feels for me and my mom. I hold her hand, 'Can I request something?'

'Sure,' she says, caressing my cheeks.

'I want to go back to my old house,' I say in a pleading tone.

'But why?' Maasi is surprised. 'The house doesn't belong to us anymore.'

'I still want to go there.'

People who go through trauma do everything in their power to forget what had happened to them and start life afresh. And here I am, whom destiny has dealt the lucky card of not being able to remember anything from my traumatic past, but all I want to do is remember more, find out more. Only a few of those haunting memories have come back so far, but now that they have, I can't just brush them off. Though Maasi has tried her best to persuade me to not dig any further into my past, I know that I have to. To know what really happened to me. To know what really happened to my mother. To let her know that her daughter hasn't just given up, that she can be as strong as her mother.

28

Nandini: Walking Into the Past

If someone had asked me a couple of weeks ago whether I was willing to go back to my old home to face the demons of my past, I would have straightaway said no. But now that I have made up my mind, I can't stop myself from going there as soon as possible. This morning, Maasi asks me again if I am sure about going there. She is afraid I might not be able to handle the hurricane of memories, especially the memories of the night the accident took place. But I know what I want now, and nothing can stop me.

There is one thing that bothers me though. I have still not revealed the whole truth to Sahil. Just thinking of what his response is going to be when he hears I'm going to Khajjiar, is making me uneasy. Somewhere in my heart I am sure he will support my decision. Hasn't he always said that he loves me and would protect me no matter what?

On our way to Khajjiar, Maasi says, 'I am doing this for you. But if you ever feel like not doing this anymore, then I'll happily turn the car around.'

'Of course,' I say to her.

The journey from Kangra to Khajjiar is done in silence. We both have a lot to think about and decide to keep to ourselves. On the way, I get a text from Sahil who wants to know about my whereabouts. I decide to tell him about my visit to Khajjiar.

Sahil: *Where are you? I have been calling you for a while.*

Me: *There's some network issue. Sorry, I didn't tell you earlier but I am going to Khajjiar.*

Sahil: *Khajjiar? Are you serious? Why? And with whom?*

Me: *I wanted to visit my old house. Maasi is driving me there.*

Sahil: *Why? What was the need to do such a thing? We had decided to start afresh. You should have at least told me before taking such a big decision.*

Me: *I needed answers, Sahil.*

Sahil: *And you think you'll get your answers there? That's all rubbish. You'll only end up hurting yourself more.*

Me: *I don't know if I will get my answers there or not. But I still want to go. If I had told you about it, you would have discouraged me from going.*

Sahil: *You're right. I would have discouraged you but only because I don't want you to get more hurt. I don't know if you'll find your answers there or not. But at least I have found my answer—You don't trust me.*

Me: *Sahil, can I ask you something?*

I wait for his reply. But I can see that he is no longer online on WhatsApp. When I don't get his response for some time, I send him another message.

Me: *Are you hiding something from me?*
He takes some time to send a reply.
Sahil: *No, I am not. Bye.*

I don't text him back after that message. He had sounded upset, and it is so easy to misunderstand someone's meaning while communicating via WhatsApp messages. I decide to explain things to Sahil after returning from Khajjiar. Right now, I am feeling, both, excitement to see my old house as well as apprehension about whether I would be able to recognise it. Whether my memories of the place would resurface, whether I'll still feel some sort of a connection with the place.

When we finally reach, I am in for a surprise. The house looks exactly the way it had looked in my flashback. The house is locked, but then so is my mind—I feel no attachment, no connection, no nostalgia associated with the place.

I had thought I would find answers to all the questions plaguing me, here. But I don't. However, I realise that it doesn't really matter, as all of this belongs to the past. Even if I don't have the house or any memories of it, I have a family. And that's all that matter.

We are standing in front of the house, just gazing at it, when I hear my name being called out.

'Nandini ...'

I turn around to see a woman, who might be a neighbour, walking towards us. She is my mother's age.

'It's good to see you again,' she says with a big smile on her face.

I feel like hiding behind Maasi because this woman clearly knows me well whereas I have no recollection of her. But Maasi doesn't let me do that. 'Hi, Mrs Sharma. How are you? I am

Nandini's aunt. We'd met when I had come for the property deal.'

She narrows her eyes, trying to recollect if they had met. 'Oh, yes, I remember. You had told me then that Nandini was unwell.' Her eyes move towards me. 'Are you feeling better now?'

'Yes,' I answer politely.

'That's great to hear.' She stares at me for some more time. 'I am sorry for your loss. Asha was such a good human being.'

'It's okay.' I am sure my short answers are annoying but I have nothing more to say.

'Why don't you come inside? Have some coffee?' She invites us to her home, and though Maasi is reluctant to accept the invitation because she can see how uncomfortable I am, Mrs Sharma insists.

We step inside her house and she directs us to the living room. Her house is similar to ours from the inside; the one I had seen in my flashbacks. Perhaps all the houses in the vicinity have a similar interior. The only difference is that Mrs Sharma's looks newly renovated. The interiors of her house look like they have been freshly painted. I am still checking out the house, when my phone, kept on the table in front of us, starts ringing. It is an unknown number, but it doesn't take me long time to realise who is calling. It's my father. Luckily, I had forgotten to save his number on my phone, otherwise Maasi would have found out that I'm in touch with him. I'm still not ready to tell her about my recent encounters with my father, so I disconnect the call instantly and put my phone on airplane mode. *Why is he calling me?* I maintain a neutral face because

I don't want Maasi to guess that I am hiding something from her. I glance at her and find that she is staring at me.

'If it's urgent, you can answer it,' she says casually.

'No problem at all.' I smile.

By then, Mrs Sharma is bringing out the coffee. After casually chatting with Maasi for some time, she moves to the time I had been in hospital and how I struggled with my health for so many months. Her eyes are brimming with sympathy.

'How are you now? I know last year couldn't have been easy for you, especially after that night when someone broke into your house.'

What did she just say? 'Someone broke into our house?'

'Yes. My husband and I had already gone to bed. But then we heard some loud noises and came outside. Before we could do or say anything, we saw you and Asha tearing away in a hurry in your car. The man, who had been in your house, got in his car too and started following you. We never got to see his face though.'

'Did the police ever find him?'

'No. Like I said, we couldn't see his face and there was no one around who could have seen him either. It was quite late by then and very dark outside.'

Maasi holds my hand and gives it a comforting squeeze as Mrs Sharma continues, 'Just leave it. It's all in the past. I'm happy to see that you have recovered and are looking perfectly healthy.'

I don't know what's happening. My body goes numb listening to Mrs Sharma's story. So, the voices I had heard and the flashbacks I had seen had been real. Someone had actually chased us. And is that same someone still following me? Does he want me to die too? But why?

After dinner, I am alone in my room pondering over what Mrs Sharma had revealed. I find no more answers despite trying hard to remember the events of that day. I am staring blankly at the ceiling fan when my phone rings. It's the same number that had called me in the afternoon—my father's. I cautiously look around to see if there is anyone hovering outside my room. Finding no one there, I pick up the call.

'Hello,' he says.

I take a few seconds to settle my nerves and then say, 'Yes, Dad.'

In a soft voice, he asks, 'Have you decided about whether you are coming with me or not?'

I had known this was coming. Ever since our meeting at the cafe, I have kept him hanging by neither rejecting nor accepting his proposal. Honestly, I still haven't made up my mind, so I say, 'Dad, I told you to give me some time to think about it. I haven't decided anything yet. It's not easy for me to leave my life here and start afresh with you.'

'Okay, as you say.' He doesn't seem too pleased by my answer. His displeasure is evident in his voice when he says, 'Take your time. But can we at least meet again?'

He probably thinks he can convince me if we meet. And it's possible he may succeed in doing so. But that's not what I want right now. My life is a mess and I need to sort it out first. I need to find out the answers to my questions.

'I'll let you know about that. I am really disturbed right now,' I finally reply.

'Why?' he asks.

For a moment, I consider whether it would be wise to reveal everything to him. But then I think, he wants to be a part of my life, so he should know everything that has happened and is still happening. My life isn't simple and straightforward and it's important I find out now whether he can handle that along with his regular life and work, before I move to Delhi. I decide to tell him.

'I just got to know what had happened with mom and me on the night of our accident.'

'What?' he reacts sharply. He wasn't expecting that.

'It wasn't an accident. Mom's death wasn't an accident.'

'What? How can you be so sure? Who told you that?' he says.

I summarise for him everything that has happened in the last few days, including recovering my lost memories and going to visit our old house. Once I finish, he takes a deep breath and says, 'Beta, if you want I can help you.'

I like that he is willing to help me out with my troubles. But I don't want him to get involved right now, especially since it would complicate things with Maasi.

'No, nothing that you need to be bothered about,' I say and I disconnect the call.

After one more restless night, I am back in college the next day. While attending a lecture, my phone vibrates. I pull it out of my pocket, thinking it must be a message from Sahil. But it turns out to be a series of pictures from an unknown number. Pictures of Maasi and me in front of my old house. Then of me entering Maasi's car outside that house. One is even of the two of us parking the car outside Maasi's house. *What the fuck is all this?* But it is the last picture that shocks me to my core. It is a picture of Sahil and me standing at the college gate. It is from today morning.

My heart starts pounding faster just looking at these pictures. Someone is clearly following me. It's frightening to think that my every move is being watched. I look around, wondering if it is someone who is in the classroom with me right now. Every person who even glances at me comes under the shadow of my suspicion. Scared, I call Sahil instantly but he doesn't answer. So, I go up to the second floor as I can't wait anymore. But Sahil isn't in his classroom either. By now I have begun to panic. I start asking his classmates about his whereabouts, but even they have no idea where he could be. Kartik is nowhere to be found either and Megha, too, isn't in college today. I keep calling Sahil again and again but there is no response from him. I text him,

Sahil, I am scared. Where are you?

I call him one more time, but meet with the same result. I feel like throwing my phone away. I start walking down the stairs, trembling out of fear. This is a familiar feeling, and I, once again, start getting flashes of memories. I can see some other pictures now, pictures on a different phone. More recent ones. Pictures of Mom, Sahil and a few other people who I don't recognise. It suddenly strikes me these are images that I must have received prior to my accident. Someone had tried to warn me earlier; clearly that someone is still trying to warn me.

My mind is still consumed with these thoughts when I feel someone's hand land on my shoulder. I let out a small shriek and turn around to see that it is Sahil.

'It's me. Don't worry.' He notices the look of terror on my face and says, 'Relax.'

I immediately start sobbing like a small child. When I hadn't been able to find him, I'd had the terrible thought that something could have happened to him because of me. Now that he is in front of me, I'm so relieved that I can't control myself. He gives me a blank expression since he still doesn't know what's wrong.

'Sahil, I don't know if you'll believe me or not. But I think I know the reason why I had disappeared from your life earlier,' I say through my tears.

We leave college in Sahil's car, and on the way, we halt at a café near my house. I tell him about my flashbacks from the day of the accident, how someone had broken into our house and then chased us when we had tried to flee from him in our car. I tell him about the pictures I have been receiving and my memories of pictures from the past which were sent to me to threaten my mom and me. I also tell him how Mom had decided that we would leave Khajjiar, only for the protection of our loved ones, out of fear that the people close to us would have to suffer because of us. 'We didn't want to put others at risk,' I finally finish.

Sahil is dumbfounded. His face progressively turns paler as he hears my story.

'What the fuck? You're saying you and your mom went through all of this alone?'

But he also finally understands why I had vanished from his life without a word. He squeezes my hand to console me.

'Nandini,' he sighs and kisses my hand, 'if you had told me all this earlier, I would have tried to support you in any way possible.'

I sense the love and warmth he feels for me through his touch. His presence is making me feel better and I tear up again. 'I am sorry. I just wanted you to be safe.'

'I know but now that we are together, no one can separate us,' he smiles at me as he says this and then hugs me.

'I know you'll always be by my side.' His words have given me confidence. 'You know what? You're the best boyfriend in this world. I regret not telling you this last time.'

He gives me a big smile. 'I love what I am hearing.'

I laugh and kiss him back.

But Sahil soon brings us back to reality. 'Someone must really have a bone to pick with you, in order to stalk you and threaten you. It must be someone you guys knew well. Can you recall his face at all?'

'My memories of him are very blurry. I have been trying to recollect his face, but I just can't.'

I feel so helpless. But Sahil reassures me, 'Relax. Don't let this affect your health.'

I love how calm Sahil is every time I get these anxiety attacks. But I still have one nagging thought. Why has he so fervently been trying to get me to move on from the past?

Was it for me, because he hadn't wanted me to relive my trauma again? Or is he related, in some way, to whatever has happened with me? His face becomes impassive every time I mention my past, and that makes me suspicious. That is one of the main reasons I still haven't told him the whole truth. But I feel that the time has come that I brush off all my suspicions about him and tell him everything that had happened that night. His earlier concern for me, when I had told him about the photographs, has given me courage and confidence. His warm embrace has given me strength to tell him the truth.

'Sahil,' I gulp and say, 'There's another thing I want to tell you.'

He raises one of his brows anxiously. 'What?'

I am still gathering my thoughts and therefore, just stare at Sahil for a while. But I can see him getting worried, so I reveal my secret—about how that man who had broken into our house had also assaulted me. I can see Sahil getting angry and agitated while I'm narrating the incident. His grip on the glass of water he is holding is so strong that I fear the glass may crack. He lowers his head and keeps staring at something on the table, occasionally looking up to glance at me. He seems to be processing the information. I can imagine many different ways in which he could react to my news, but what he finally says crushes my heart.

'Are you sure all this happened? You could have been hallucinating.'

On hearing this, my heart drops to my stomach and I stare at him in shock. I had gone through a terrible assault on the day of that accident and had dealt with the related trauma all by myself, and instead of supporting me, Sahil is refusing to believe me.

'No, I wasn't,' I tell him sternly. I place my hand on his and say, 'Sahil, it has taken a lot of courage for me to tell you this. It was not a hallucination.'

'It could be. How can you be so sure? I don't want to argue about this any more.'

I am in complete disbelief. I had never expected that Sahil would behave in such a manner. It feels as if he has gone back to being the earlier version of himself from my first days in college—the one who was angry with me, and wouldn't talk to me, and was mean to me all the time. I had thought that if I told him the whole truth, he would become even more protective about me. I had believed that the truth wouldn't make any difference to our relationship, but the exact opposite had happened. *Why?*

'I thought you'll ...' I start but can't get the words out. After taking a deep breath, I lean towards him with a sigh. Wiping away my tears myself, I say, 'You said you'll stand by me and support me no matter what happens. And now when I need you the most, this is your reaction. This is you supporting me?' My eyes are pleading with him, asking him to understand my hurt.

But Sahil is unmoved. Instead, he says tersely, 'Okay, enough of that. You've spouted a lot of nonsense this far and I have supported you through all of it. But this? This is too much.' He stands up from the chair and pushes my hand away. 'Stop digging into your past. It's time you decided. Either you stay in your past or you be with me.' He picks up his phone from the table and leaves with one final parting blow. 'Call me once you have made up your mind. Till then stay away from me.'

Sahil doesn't even look back as he walks away, leaving me completely devastated. I have weathered a lot of shocks over the last few months, but what has happened today has shattered me. I keep sitting at the table staring at my hands. And my mind goes back to Rudra's words from earlier,

Sahil is not the right person for you. He's not protecting you; he's dangerous.

I could hear my inner voice laughing at me.

Nandini, weren't you convinced that Sahil loves you and cares for you deeply.

29

Nandini: Broken Pieces, Unsolved Puzzles

I keep calling Sahil again and again for the rest of the day, but he doesn't answer any of my calls. He also doesn't come to college the next day. I am tempted to ask Rudra what he had meant when he had called Sahil dangerous. But I'm still not sure if he can be trusted. Apart from the devastation I feel at Sahil's reaction, I also cannot stop myself from suspecting that Sahil was involved in my accident in some way. I have never asked Sahil the hard questions because it has been easier this way. All these past months, Sahil has continuously asked me for reassurance that I would not leave him; I had never thought that *he* would leave me instead. It seems I am back in the same place where I had been, right after being discharged from the hospital—lost, hopeless and clueless. The only difference between then and now is that some of my memory is back.

In the early days of getting back together with Sahil, I had wanted to ask him several times why he still wanted to be with me when I had been the one who had broken his heart. But I never got down to asking him, because I was so happy and grateful that he wanted to be with me in spite of everything, especially since he could be with any girl he wanted. When he had asked me to not dwell on the past, I had believed that it was because of the pain I had caused him.

Nandini, you don't need to worry or force yourself to remember why we broke up. His words had reassured me.

The first time I had met Sahil after my accident, I had been confused and guilty because he had told me that I had broken up with him and put him through a lot of misery. But once we had become a couple again, I also became the focus of all his attention. I never gave credence to my suspicions about Sahil because I felt that I could implicitly trust him. Every moment spent with him had made me love him more. I had even started believing that he was the strong pillar that would bring the much-needed balance in my life. In my mind, Sahil and I had been one person, who wanted to share their lives together. Even when I had told him that I wasn't his old Nandini anymore, Sahil had been adamant that it didn't matter to me. His words are still echoing in my head.

Trust me, you might have forgotten everything but you haven't forgotten yourself. I am sure of this by the way you kissed me yesterday, the way you care for everyone around you, it's all you. The old Nandini. You should embrace life once again. You deserve that because you are the best. It's time to be brave—to not just face life like you are doing right now but to also embrace it with open arms. I want you to always remember that no matter where you are in life, no matter how low you have fallen, no matter how bleak the situation seems, that is NOT THE END. This is not the end of your story. This is not the end of our story.

But, it seems Sahil and my story had ended a long time ago. Had I been deluded? Had Sahil been lying to me all this while, faking how worried he was about me?

I realise now, that the arms that once made me feel secure have abandoned me. Sahil had brought me to life, only to kill me again.

I continue the rest of my day as if nothing has happened. After college, Kartik and Megha meet me at the college gate and ask, 'Have you and Sahil had a fight? Is everything all right?'

'Yes.' I fake a smile. 'Everything's fine.'

I leave without saying anything more to them. It is difficult for me to hide my feelings from them. Even after reaching home, I directly go to my room without speaking to anyone. I have just settled down on the bed when I hear the sound of glass shattering. I rush out and see Maasi standing near the dining table staring blankly at her phone. Even Rashi comes running out of her room to see what has happened. We exchange a glance and then, look back at Maasi. That's when I notice the broken window glass scattered all around her. Someone has attacked the house. *Again.*

'Maasi, are you okay?' I say. 'What happened?'

She doesn't look up from her phone. Her hands are shaking and her face has a horrified expression. Looking at her, I feel terrified too.

'Mom, say something...' Rashi stammers, 'I am calling Papa right away.'

I walk up to Maasi, avoiding the glass pieces, and she shows me her phone. On it are pictures of me leaving the college; even one of me from today when I had been speaking with Megha and Kartik at the college gate. I see that a piece of paper is wrapped around the stone lying on the floor, the one that had shattered the glass. I pick it up and read what is written on it.

Don't mess with me. Another warning.

Maasi snatches the paper from me, her terrified face turning furious. 'These pictures ...'

I sighed, 'I know. Even I have received similar pictures.'

Unlike me, Maasi doesn't take the warning lightly. She takes me to the police station the next morning itself. When we enter the station, all the benches and chairs in the waiting area are occupied, so we stand waiting for our turn. In some time, we are asked to come inside. We sit in front of one of the police officers.

Inspector V.K. Bhatia – I read his name from the badge pinned to his chest.

He is in his mid-forties, is heavily built and has a thick moustache and a beer belly. Maasi shows him all the photos we have received and gives him the threatening note that had been thrown inside our house last night. She also gives him the phone number from which we had received the messages. While Maasi explains my case to the officer in detail, the officer drinks his tea and fiddles with his phone. Occasionally, he glances at us to show that he is paying attention and is interested in helping us out. However, that isn't true. Instead of writing down the complaint, he first turns to me and says, 'You girls roam on the streets late at night these days. You drink and party with all sorts of friends, and then you come here to harass us.'

I feel like punching his face, but Maasi is more patient and tells him about my medical history. That's when he sits up and actually pays attention. 'When did all this start?' he asks.

'The last couple of days,' Maasi answers.

The officer looks at me, probably realising that I want to say something too. Before he can ask me, I clarify, 'Actually, not just the last couple of days.' Maasi immediately turns her head towards me. 'I feel someone has been stalking me for quite a number of days.'

I can see that Maasi is shocked, but she doesn't say anything to me and shifts her attention back to the officer, who is asking another question, 'Do you have any suspects in mind? Anyone you know who would do something like this?'

'No,' Maasi responds.

The officer looks at me as if I might have something to add again. Though I do suspect someone, I don't want to take his name. I can't. I still love him, even though he seems like a stranger now.

'No,' I reply. Maasi visibly relaxes on hearing this.

'Any boyfriend or ex-boyfriend?' the policeman asks. I narrow my eyes. His tone is extremely annoying and he has just assumed that I am someone who must have a boyfriend. He sees that I am not pleased with the question. 'Madam, in most of these cases, the culprit is either the boyfriend or the ex-lover.'

Before Maasi can take Sahil's name, I answer, 'No. There's nothing of that sort.'

He simply nods and says, 'Okay. We will get back to you in a few days after conducting our investigation.'

'What investigation?' Maasi is furious, 'You mean till then we should continue to live in fear while this person roams freely around us?'

'Madam, we can't provide security to everyone who comes here with a complaint.' He keeps his phone aside and stares at us as if we are annoying him. 'Chaturvedi, inki complaint likhle,' he yells.

Maasi asks, 'How long do you think it will take you to catch him?'

The policeman laughs and again asks his colleague to write our complaint. We complete the paperwork and get back into the car.

'Do you think these cops will really help us?' I ask, still annoyed by his behaviour.

'We don't have an option, Nandini.' Maasi sighs, 'But you please be careful.'

I nod. Maasi drives ahead for a few feet and then pulls over on the side of the road. She is teary-eyed. 'What happened, Maasi?' I ask, concerned.

The moment I ask her, she lets out a sob and tears start falling from her eyes. She leans towards me and gives me a hug. 'I wish I had known what was happening in Asha's life. I would have helped her. I regret not being on good terms with her in her last days.'

I, too, wish we could go back in time and mend things. 'You're already doing everything you can for her daughter,' I say.

The ache in my heart is not physiological, although it does feel that way sometimes. I am still in trauma, not having got over the incident that had changed my life and taken my mother away from me. I also feel guilty that I have put everyone around me in danger.

After dinner that evening, I get a call from Sahil.

'I need to see you right now. I am waiting at the bus stop. Come if you want to talk,' he says hurriedly. It sounds less like a request and more like a command.

My heart skips a beat on hearing his voice after more than twenty-four hours of radio silence. I wonder how it is that even after everything that has happened—him reacting so badly to what I told him, not speaking to me afterwards and my suspecting that Sahil had something to do with my accident—he can still have such a powerful effect on me. But too much has happened since yesterday, and Maasi is worried for my safety. It isn't possible to leave the house right now to meet him.

'I can't come right now, Sahil. Maasi won't allow me to do that,' I reply.

There is silence from his side and I think the call has got disconnected. I look at the screen, but the call is still going on.

'Hello, you there?' I ask, to confirm whether he still wants to talk.

'Fine. Don't come. I'll just assume you don't love me and don't want to repair our relationship. Let's end this thing forever.'

Had he called me to try to patch things up with me? Was he feeling sorry for what he had done yesterday? I am not sure what I should do, but eventually my heart wins over my mind.

'Okay, I'll come,' I say, and he disconnects the call.

If I'd tried to get permission from Maasi to go out to meet Sahil, there was no way she would have given it. The only option left to me is to quietly sneak out of the house. After dinner, Maasi, Uncle and Rashi, usually watch television in their rooms. Which is how I succeed in leaving the house a few minutes later without anyone noticing me. I have already decided that I won't stay for very long, only enough to hear what Sahil has to say.

As I am walking towards the bus stop, I hear someone call out my name. I turn around and see a black Innova pull up. I walk over to the car, assuming that Sahil must have come to the bus stop in someone else's car. But suddenly someone grips me from behind. Instinctively, I push away that person, and try to run away. However, whoever it is manages to catch me before I can go very far. He holds his hand over my mouth preventing me from yelling for help.

Damn! I shouldn't have come.

'Who are you?' I ask in a muffled voice, since his hand is still covering my mouth.

He lowers his head to my ear and whispers, 'You were warned.'

Goosebumps break out all over my body and I use all my strength to scream for help. But his hand is clamped tightly over my mouth, and all that comes out is a muffled sound. He hurls me into the back seat of the car, which quickly speeds away. I can see a masked man in the front seat driving the car. The other person, who had caught me and pushed me inside the car, is sitting next to me and is also wearing a mask. The car is hurtling along deserted streets. Suddenly, everything goes dark and I realise that the man has blindfolded me.

I feel as if I have walked onto the set of a bad television show. But in my case, there is no hero here who can save me from the bad guys.

30

Nandini: Done and Dusted

After what seems like hours of driving, the car finally comes to a halt. Someone picks me up, drags me from the car into a room inside a house, and then drops me on the floor. I hit the ground hard and feel pain shooting through my body. Someone opens my blindfold and I blink several times to find my bearings. As I am doing that, someone grabs me by my shoulders and pulls me up into a sitting position.

'Ugh ...' I groan as I lift my head and finally manage to look around.

Where am I? Why am I here? And, more importantly, where is Sahil?

All these questions are racing through my mind. I am feeling slightly dizzy and disoriented, as if I have just woken up from a slumber. The last thing I can remember is someone blindfolding me inside the car. As I start to regain the use of my senses, panic settles in. I try to stand up, but I am unable to move my limbs. I looked down to see my hands and legs tied together tightly with a thick rope.

My phone isn't anywhere near me. I scream as loudly as I can but no one can hear me. The place is completely desolate.

I should have listened to Maasi. She told me to be extra careful. Yet I sneaked out. I believed Sahil even when my gut instinct was telling me that there was something wrong about him. I am sure he is the one who has brought me here. After all, he's the only one who didn't want me to remember my past. Maybe all this is connected with what had happened earlier. Maybe his powerful dad is involved.

I look around the room, which is completely empty except for me, a chair, and a flickering lightbulb hanging from the ceiling. The single wooden door to the room is in the corner and is shut. My throat feels tired from all the screaming. I can hear the sound of a distant thud echoing across the cold, hard floor. Someone is coming. The door swings open. A tall, muscular man walks into the room, pulls the chair in front of me and sits in it to face me. I narrow my eyes to look at him properly. The streetlight from the window behind me is falling on his face. I can see an unfamiliar face with a lot of messy hair.

'Who are you and what do you want?' I try hard to recognise him, but it seems this is the first time I have seen him.

I scream again, hoping for someone to come to my rescue.

'Sssh ...' He comes closer to me. 'There's no point in screaming. Don't waste your energy. We are far away from Kangra and no one ever comes to this warehouse.'

A blanket of hopelessness envelopes me. My mind races to the worst-case scenario. If what he is saying is true, then it is unlikely I'll be saved.

'What do you want? I don't even know you.' I repeat my question.

He moves closer and grabs my chin roughly, 'You really don't remember me?'

'No ... I don't,' I stammer

He gives me a sinister smile, 'But you're starting to remember, aren't you. And that's a problem. I have been watching you.'

Watching me? Is he the one who has been stalking me? The one who followed me on the back road, the one who stood outside the hospital door, the one who was sending all those pictures? Is he that person? I know I need to escape from this place as quickly as I can, but I'm not leaving until I find out his motive. Is he is related to Sahil? If he is, then does the fact that I was in a relationship with Sahil mean that I was with someone who had known about the assault on me that night as well as the car accident that had followed.

'I seriously don't know you.' I plead with him to let me go.

'I would have let you go.' He pushes my chin down, removing his hand. I jerk back and try to steady myself. It is painful, but he seems to be enjoying himself. 'But it's always better to get rid of the problem itself rather than to keep dealing with the trouble that the problem is capable of causing. Especially when you know the problem has the ability to destroy you.'

I smile sarcastically, realising that beneath that intimidating demeanour is a man who is scared that I might destroy him. 'Good to see your fear. I like it,' I say.

He sighs and then, gets up to kick me hard. His sinister smile is back. 'You are exactly like your mother. Your resilience, your determination ... trying to act smarter than you are for no reason.' He looks straight into my eyes and whispers, 'And your father hated all of it.'

My eyes widen. I'm not sure I have heard him right.

'My father?' My voice splutters.

'Yes, your father. I work for him. I am his business associate. I have been working with him for the last 20 years,' the man continues.

'Does he know you have brought me here forcefully?' I spit out while still struggling to release my hands and legs.

'Let me tell you one thing. Nothing happens here without his permission. Nothing.'

So, it is my father who has been behind all this! My own father? The man who had behaved so nicely with me at the café just a few days ago? The one who is trying to convince me about his desire to reunite with his daughter? That same man has been doing all this. How can he be so ruthless? How can he do this to his own daughter? And my mother, the woman he claims to have loved, was he behind her death too? I am filled with disgust just thinking about him.

But that means Sahil is innocent! How foolish of me to have suspected him. All he had ever wanted was to protect me. He had known that my father was dangerous, but I hadn't listened to him. And now, here I am, sitting with this bastard who has abducted me on my father's instructions.

'We had never wanted to do all this. If your mother had agreed peacefully and if you had kept your mouth shut that night, things would have been so different. What did your father ever want from either of you? Just for the two of you to go live with him. He had found you both after so many years and all he had wanted was to be with you. But no, your mother had a huge ego. She wasn't ready to accept him back, she wanted to expose him.'

He stands up from his chair and starts pacing in front of me. I look around me again, hoping to find a way to escape from here, but I don't find anything that can help me.

Suddenly, we hear the sound of another pair of shoes walking towards the room. I silently watch as someone walks up to the goon in front of me. It's dark, but I can see his face with the help of the streetlight.

It's my father!

31

Nandini: Losing Hope

Trust me, I am a changed man now and want a chance to be your father again. As soon as I see my father's face, I remember what he said to me a few days ago at the café. I feel numb. Even my mind that usually works overtime has nothing more to think. I feel so foolish for believing him. How I wish I had heeeded the warnings of all my loved ones and not gone to meet him. I can only feel anger and despair. He is standing in front of me and we are both staring at each other. I have never known what a father-daughter relationship bond feels like, but in this moment, all I can think is that if a father is someone as sick as mine, then it is better to be an orphan.

'Is this the way you want to mend things with me? To be my father again? By using your fake tears and emotions to sway me? By abducting *me*?' I ask furiously. I am pretending to be strong even though I am completely petrified.

'You know, your mother worked as my father's secretary 20 years ago? I told you about that,' he finally speaks up. His voice is calm and composed, and I feel nauseated just looking at him. 'She was an intelligent, smart and confident girl and before I knew what was happening, I fell in love with her. We were separated because of my parent's wishes. After that, I genuinely tried to find her again for years but couldn't.' His face shows remorse, but this time I am not falling for it. 'And then one day, many years later, I saw your mother in Khajjiar working at a school where I had been invited as a chief guest. I was shocked to see her sitting in the front row. My Asha! It didn't take me long to realise that my love for her hadn't diminished over the years. Now that I had met her again, I wanted her back in my life. I even asked her to come with me to Delhi. We would have built a new life together, but she betrayed me.'

The more he speaks, the angrier I get. I can't hold myself back anymore and shout at him, 'She didn't betray you. In fact, it was you who never deserved her love. Because you are sick. Maasi has been right about you all along.'

In an instant, he raises his hand and slaps me hard. But then he starts apologising immediately as if hadn't wanted to hit me. 'I am sorry for that. But didn't your mother teach you any manners? Is that the way to speak to your father?'

His associate doesn't move an inch, he just stands there looking at us silently. My father's slap really scares me. I'm no longer sure what he is capable of doing. Both these men have total control over me, especially since my hands and legs are tied.

Maybe he will kill me too. Like he killed my mother.

Seeing that I am not talking back to him anymore, he sighs and says, 'That's better.' Then he continues, 'I had given your mother a few days to decide. I wanted a positive response from her. But instead of coming along with me quietly, she started digging into my work, into some shady dealings that I'd had with some local politicians. She had even managed to find some stuff that she had thought she could blackmail me with, to keep me away from you and her. What was the need to do all that? We could have all lived happily together in Delhi. But your mother was hell bent on being unreasonable.'

I finally know why Mom had left Delhi all those years ago and had never informed my father about her whereabouts. It is possible she was trying to hide us from my father and his family until he finally gave up.

'She never contacted me again,' my father continues, not waiting for a response from me. 'She hadn't wanted you to know about me and my family which is why she never shared all this with you. She told me as much the one time she agreed to meet me in Khajjiar. She told me about the information she had collected against me and threatened to share that with the media if I didn't agree to stay away from both of you. But I couldn't have her doing that now, could I? I intend to contest the assembly elections this year. Such news could have destroyed my entire political career.'

I've had enough of his explanations. I don't care what he has to say. 'Please just let me go. No one will ever get to know about all this. I don't even know what information you are talking about. I won't say a word to anyone. Please just let me live my life.' I pretend to be helpless, hoping to persuade a father's heart to show his daughter some mercy. But my father remains unmoved.

He gets a call from someone. Once he is done, he starts walking away from me and instructs his so-called colleague to accompany him.

As he is leaving, he says one last thing to me. 'I hope you know that there's no point in you shouting here. No can come to help you. Just sit here quietly until we return.'

By now, my arms and legs are paining badly from having been tied for such a long time. I try to distract my mind, by thinking about everything my father has told me tonight. It is clear to me that his love for my mother was a sick kind of love, a love that had resulted in her death. And for that, my father deserved to go to jail. I needed to get out of here if only to make sure that my mother got justice.

I am glad my ploy has worked so far. My father and his henchman have both assumed that I have lost all my strength to fight and that I wouldn't dare to escape from here. Now I just have to think of a plan before they come back to the room. I have very little time to make my escape.

I scrutinise the room I am in. It's a warehouse that seems to have been abandoned for a while since there is dust everywhere. Apart from a single flickering bulb, there are no lights inside. I can see things around only because of the streetlight pouring into the room through the window behind me. The glass pane of the window is almost completely broken, except for a long shard that is sticking out from the lower edge of the window sill.

A window with a broken glass! I can use that!

I drag myself closer to the window and manage to stand up after several clumsy attempts. I try to cut the rope that is tying my hands by running it against the edge of the shard. In the process, I end up cutting my skin too. Blood from my hands is dripping down but eventually the rope gives away. I quickly untie the rope binding my legs and look around to see how

I can escape. The door is still shut and there is no sign of my father or his associate. I have to make a break from this place right now.

There's no way to climb out of the window with the sharp shard of glass jutting out. I would only end up injuring myself if I tried that. Instead, I try to open the window but the lock seems to be rusted and it doesn't budge. Frustrated, I let out a small shriek before I realise what I have done.

It's over now. They must've heard me. How could I be so stupid to scream? There's no way I'll be able to escape from here now. I turn around to see my father's associate running towards me and fear engulfs me. My father is following him. I keep trying to pull at the lock but it's no use. My father has reached up to me now and raises his hand and slaps me hard. The last thing I feel is the sting of his slap and then I fall into darkness.

32

Nandini: The Final Triumph

When I come to, I realise that my hands and legs have been tied back again, the ropes stinging me sharply where I had cut my hands earlier. I keep my eyes closed and start thinking.

Is there any way to get out of here? Some way to contact Maasi and tell her about my location? But I don't even know where I am. All I have been told is that I'm somewhere in the outskirts of Kangra. There's no way anyone would ever be able to find me here. Even Maasi will realise I'm missing only after she wakes up in the morning. By then, it might be too late.

My father sits in the chair in front of me and lights a cigarette. I still don't know why he is holding me here. Does he think that I know something about the information my mother had collected against him? Or that I know where it could be kept? Or does he intend to kill me so that I'm no longer a threat to him or his political ambitions. Is it possible that a father would kill his own daughter only to ensure his victory in the next assembly elections? I have no answers to these questions.

But I do have some questions for my father. 'Why weren't there any legal consequences of what had happened the night my mom died? Even your associate wasn't jailed, right?'

'The perks of being a rich businessman,' my father says with a smirk. 'Everything in this world is for sale if the price is right.'

Ah! I get it now. They had paid the right price to get the CCTV footage outside our house destroyed. No wonder they managed to escape.

'And how much did you pay for letting him sexually assault your own daughter?' I glare at him.

'That never happened,' he replies continuing to smoke casually. I had wanted to trigger a father's instinct to protect their child, by asking that question. But my father has just brushed aside the question.

This world is so cruel. I think to myself. *This awful, disgraceful man who claims to be my father is still alive while my innocent mother who always tried to protect me is dead.*

My father's associate speaks up, 'My job that day was to get the evidence from your mother by hook or by crook. But your mother would not hand it to me no matter what I said. As for you, I had merely overpowered you but I never raped you. It was just to make sure you stopped shouting while I was dealing with your mother. That's why I had pushed you down on the sofa. But you hit me and tried to escape with your mother in the car. It's not my fault that your car crashed and your mother died.'

I don't know if I should believe him. My memories tell a different story and I would rather trust them than this goon.

My father joins in then. 'And now that your memories are returning, you can prove dangerous for my political career. That is why I had wanted you to be under my roof so that I could always keep an eye on you.' He gives me a remorseful look. 'We could have lived together happily. But fate had other plans.'

If I had a gun with me right now, I would have shot him dead. Instead, I sigh and gather up all my strength to say, 'Why don't you just kill me like you killed my mother? I don't want to hear anything you say anymore. Just get rid of me.'

'Nandini! I didn't kill your mother. I would never do that. It was an accident.'

'Even if it was an accident, you are the person behind it. You forced us to run away. It's to escape you that we were in a car that crashed. And I'm sure even if the car hadn't crashed, you would have found some other way to kill my mother,' I say through gritted teeth.

'Believe whatever you want.' With that he brushes off my allegations. His phone rings again and he walks away to pick it up. His associate follows him.

I can hear them talk in a faint whisper. 'I need to go for an urgent meeting. Don't do anything till I return. And keep an eye on her.' With that, he leaves.

It's been an hour or so that my father left. His associate has also left the room assuming that I pose no threat. In the meantime, while pretending to be asleep, I have slowly been loosening the rope binding my hands. The associate had not tied the knots carefully the second time round and I have managed to open them. Phew! I breathe a sigh of relief.

Nandini, you have another chance! I say to myself.

I quickly check to confirm that no one is around, and I run towards the window. I try again to open the window but the lock is still jammed. I keep going at it, occasionally turning around to make sure that the door to the room is still closed. I realise no matter how hard I try, I won't be able to unlock the window. So, I ram my elbow into the remaining shard of glass, shattering it. As I am clearing away the glass, one piece pierces my palm, but I don't care about the pain anymore. I have to get out of here. With one last look at the entrance, I am ready to climb out of the window. But as I put my foot on the sill, I hear footsteps and my heart stops.

Fuck, I need to rush.

The footsteps are coming closer and my anxiety is increasing. In spite of that, I somehow manage to climb onto the window sill. The window is at least one storey high, but I have no option so I jump. My body crashes to the ground with a loud thud. A stone lying on the ground manages to pierce my back as I land. It's a miracle I haven't cried out from the pain. It is dark all around me. The shadows of the trees surrounding the warehouse are making creepy patterns on the ground. But I don't pause even for a second. I get to my feet and start running as fast as I can, down the long driveway from the warehouse to the road. I constantly expect to hear someone running after me or to fire a gun at me, but nothing happens. I reach the end of the driveway after running for at least half a kilometre. Once I am on the road, I look at both sides, hoping to see a car that could help me. But the road is empty. I stand there for a while with my hands on my knees, trying to catch a breath. Suddenly, a hand clamps down on my father while another pulls my body back. I struggle with all my might, hitting whoever it is repeatedly, pushing my elbows back into the person's stomach in order to escape. It's then I hear a familiar voice, 'Nandini, will you stop? Its me.'

I turn around. 'Sahil?' I sigh and collapse in his arms.

33

Nandini: Last Nail in the Coffin?

It is Sahil! I have never felt such relief in my life. I want to bury myself in his arms and never be parted from him. But then I remember that I am trying to escape my captors. I fear my father's associate must have closed the distance between us by now. Out of breath, I tell Sahil, 'It's my father. He's the one behind all this. He's the one who attacked my mother and me on the night of our accident. He is the one who has been stalking and intimidating me.'

Sahil rubs my back to calm me down. I am still trying to catch my breath, holding onto my knees. 'It's okay, just relax,' he tells me. I hear the sound of a siren coming closer and realise that the police must be on its way. 'The cops will handle the rest,' Sahil says.

The perks of being a rich businessman! I suddenly remember my father's words. I look at Sahil with dread in my eyes and words rush out of my mouth in a panic. 'You shouldn't have told the cops. They are of no use. He and his associate managed to get away the last time with their help.'

'Nandini...' he shakes me by my shoulders. 'Please calm down. He won't escape this time.' His voice has an assuring quality to it. I wonder at his confidence. Then he says with a smile, 'Have you forgotten? My father is an equally rich businessman.'

I remember that Sahil had told me that his father was a politician too and was the owner of many businesses. Probably he is also an influential man. But can it be as simple as Sahil says it will be?

'Are you sure?' I want him to reassure me. 'What if he manages to escape again and comes back to harass me after lying low for some time?'

'He is not going to escape again.' He pulls me into his embrace. 'Please for now, let the police handle everything. Okay?'

A police car comes to a screeching stop in front of us and a couple of officers hurry over to where we are standing. Neither of them is the cop, my Maasi and I had spoken to at the police station.

It's then that Sahil tells me, 'Dad has called the Superintendent of Police just for this case. So, you can trust these officers.'

I nod. I don't want to repeat my earlier mistake of not trusting him. 'But how did you guys find me? I initially thought it was you ...,' I trail off.

He looks at me sharply and say, 'You thought I was the one who had kidnapped you, didn't you? Because it was me who had called you to meet at the bus stop.'

'I am sorry,' I say, regret filling my heart.

'It's fine Nandini. Don't be sorry.' He smiles and explains himself, 'I waited for you for some time near the bus stop. When you didn't come, I thought you must have decided not to meet me and I started to leave. But then I saw Rashi standing at the bus stop and I asked her about you. That's how she got to know that I was there to meet you but you had not showed up. Finally, she left and soon after, so did I, convinced that you weren't going to come. An hour later, I was at home and I got a call from Rashi saying you were not at home either. That's when warning bells started ringing in my mind. I knew something was wrong. Fortunately, my dad was at home, so I went and told him everything, including how you had disappeared. He immediately called the SP who started tracking your phone. They also had a look at the CCTV footage of the area from where you were abducted. They managed to track down the car. From there, it didn't take us very long to find you.'

I hug him again while Sahil says, 'The entire process was fast-tracked because my father considers you to be a part of our family.'

'So, now I am the one taking advantage of his position?' I say with a smile, making Sahil laugh.

'Nandini this has now become a high profile case!' he smirks. 'So now no one would believe anything your father says. We have all the evidence and witnesses we need to get him convicted.'

'I just want all this to be over,' I cry out.

'It will be. It's just a matter of time now—let the police get their hands on him.' Sahil wipes my tears away and says, 'By the way, if Rashi hadn't told me about you, all this would not have been possible.'

I still can't believe that Rashi had something to do with my rescue.

'She not only told me that you were missing, but also insisted that I find you somehow. She was really concerned about you, I could hear it in her voice. She had been worried for you ever since someone threw a stone inside your home.'

I smile. Whatever Sahil may say, I know better that it isn't that incident that spurred Rashi's concern for me. That process had started much earlier. But I don't say anything to him. *Sometimes it's better to let go of things. Probably that's the best way to remain happy and have a healthy relationship.* Megha had been so right. I sigh thinking about all that has happened. I smile and thank my stars that Rashi informed Sahil at the right time.

One of the officers greets me, 'Are you okay? Your family will be here any minute.'

'I am fine.'

I briefly tell him everything that had happened since the moment of my abduction. I also give them the associate's description and direct them towards the warehouse.

'Don't worry, we will get him,' the police officer assures us.

One police team immediately goes towards the warehouse to track the associate down while the other stays with us. After a few minutes, I see Maasi's car approaching. As soon as the car stops, before even the headlights go off, Maasi rushes out of the car along with Uncle and Rashi.

'Are you okay, Nandini?' She scans me from top to bottom, panic evident in her voice. 'We just got to know your father is behind all this. That bastard ... this time we'll make sure he doesn't get away scot-free.' Seeing my bruises, tears roll down her eyes and she takes me into her arms.

'I am fine, Maasi,' I say, holding on to her. She means so much to me that I have no words to express my feelings.

Uncle gently pats my head and says, 'Thank god you are safe. We were all so scared.'

I smile at him and then shift my gaze to Rashi who has been looking at me intently from a distance.

I let go of Maasi and walk towards Rashi. I can see the remorse on her face for everything bad she has ever said about me or done to me. 'I am sorry Nandini. For everything. Please forgive me.'

'You don't need to be sorry,' I say. For the first time, I see a smile on her face that is meant just for me. 'Rather, I should thank you for informing Sahil in time. If it wasn't for you, I would have still been running in the woods, trying to escape from those evil men. Who knows, maybe I would have even been dead by now.'

Time has a wonderful way of showing us what really matters in life. Rashi instantly hugs me and starts sobbing. Her gesture makes me emotional too and brings tears to my eyes. A sister's love is always so special. No matter the distance, no matter the differences, no matter the issues, once a sister always a sister!

This isn't the ideal place for a family reunion, nonetheless it feels like one, especially with Sahil being here to.

The police officer who had stayed behind with us suggests to Maasi, 'Why don't you take Nandini to the hospital so that they can treat her bruises? I'll send one of my officers with you, just in case. And don't worry, we'll handle things here and I assure you, we'll catch the culprit.'

'Sure,' Maasi says with a nod. 'Thank you, officer.'

Maasi and Uncle guide us to the car. Sahil comes along with us as well. Even though we have left the place but my thoughts keep straying back there. Despite all the reassurances given by Sahil and the Himachal Pradesh Police, my mind won't feel calm until my father gets caught.

Before we reach the hospital, Maasi gets a call on her phone. It's the police officer calling to say, 'The associate has been caught. And he has confessed to everything. Harshvardhan Chowdhary, too, will be behind bars within the next 24 hours.'

Maasi's phone is on speaker, so when I hear the news, I almost jump out of my seat in happiness. I still can't believe that I actually managed to escape my captors. It is such a satisfying feeling. This time, everything around me feels like the calm that comes after a big storm. Everything has settled down and even though there has been some destruction, I know the worst is over. After all, the sun always shines after a storm. In the same way, the joy that comes after pain, is even more heart-warming!

34

Nandini: Sunshine after the Storm

The next morning, my father's name is all over the headlines.

Harshvardhan Chowdhary arrested for kidnapping his own daughter. Another criminal-turned-wannabe politician!

Chowdhury group hides their illegal activities behind shell companies!

Delhi police seizes records of more than 20 shell companies and foreign accounts in the name of Harshvardhan Chowdhary!

HC group shares tank by 40 per cent in light of the owner's arrest!

Nowhere is it mentioned that it was Sahil's dad, Mr Avasthi, who had helped the police expose my father. Last night, after returning from the hospital, I had told the police everything my father had told me at the warehouse—his relationship with my mother, how my mother had wanted him to stay away from us, the evidence she had about his illegal activities. We eventually managed to find even the evidence my mom had gathered, saved in a pen drive kept in the old box that Maasi had handed over to me when I had first come to live with her. My father's fate is now sealed and I have no words to express how content I am. I am sure even my mother is smiling from the heavens.

'Why didn't you believe me when I told you about what happened on the night of our accident?' I ask Sahil a few days later. We are in his car driving to a place which is supposed to be a surprise for me. 'You left that day without any explanation.'

He turns his head towards me and pulls me close. 'I am sorry I didn't believe you. I was in denial because it pained me to know that someone had assaulted you that night and that I hadn't been there to protect you. It was easier for me to believe that you must have been hallucinating. But that was wrong on my part. Please forgive me.' He kisses my hand. I smile at Sahil, finally understanding him, and he looks visibly relieved. 'Also, when I told you to not dwell on your past, my intention was just to make sure that your past didn't trouble you anymore. I wanted you to live in the present. I felt that the way you ruminated over the past all the time wasn't healthy. I wanted to see you happy and joyful and I wanted you to embrace the second chance that life had given you and us, instead of looking back into the past.'

I listen to him thoughtfully. He isn't wrong. With the amount I was thinking about my past, I hadn't really embraced my new life. 'I understand what you are saying but my happiness was stuck in the past. And I knew that until I faced it, I would never be content again.' I sigh and play with the lock of hair that keeps falling on his forehead. 'You know what,' I tell him,

'I thought you didn't want to be with me anymore because of the assault.'

Sahil immediately stops the car on the side of the road and tightens his grip on my hand. 'Later when I thought about what you had told me, about everything that you had gone through all alone, I was very upset. I cursed myself for not reassuring you when you told me your horrible news, because that's when you had needed me the most. That's what I wanted to tell you when I had called you to the bus stop.' He kisses my forehead, 'But from now on, I promise, I'll always be with you. Now and forever.'

True love isn't about someone wanting to spend their good times with you. It's about the person being with you in your bad times, suffering along with you, trying to pull you out of your misery. And that's what Sahil has done for me. If there was only one gift I could give him in life, I would give him the ability to see himself through my eyes so that he can realise how precious he is to me!

We finally reached our destination. I realise Sahil has brought me to the Bajreshwari temple. I'm glad we are here, even though I hadn't asked Sahil to bring me here. This time I don't run inside, instead I walk along with Sahil. This time, there is also no pain, regret or melancholy, just contentment, love and faith. After seeking the Goddess's blessings, I once again go to stand in front of the marble stone which has my mother's name carved on it.

Asha Kashyap.

I read the name again and I can't control my tears anymore. The only difference this time is that these are happy tears. 'Mom, I miss you so much. I have become a strong girl. Not as strong as you, but, I hope, enough to make you proud. The person responsible for your death is now behind bars.'

I can feel the same positive aura around the stone that I had felt the first time I had come here with Maasi. Once again, I can feel my mother's strong presence around me. The last time I had come, I'd had no memories of her and I had so badly wanted to recollect them so that I could know how much she had loved me. Today, I know I am the person she had loved the most in the world. I close my eyes and thank God for everything. The way Maasi has stood by me and made me feel like a part of her family. She has become a second mother to me. Rashi is right; Maasi knows everything there is to know about me—my likes, dislikes, my wants and even my feelings. Isn't a mother supposed to know all that?

Last night Rashi and I had our first ever sister-talk since the accident. I told her more about me and how I felt about Maasi. This time she didn't get angry. She has finally accepted me not just as her sister but also as her mother's daughter. And Uncle, with his quiet support, is the strongest pillar of our family and I am happy to have a father figure like him in my life.

If Maasi has given me my life back, Sahil has given my life purpose. Without him, life would be meaningless. I feel that my life is complete because he is there. And the circle gets completed by the friendships I share with Megha and Kartik, who bring the much-needed joy and laughter to my life. Even last night, they had come to meet me in the hospital. Megha's first statement had been, 'Nandini, you're alive ... I'm so glad. I thought you were gone with the wind, leaving me all alone, with no one to bitch about Kartik with.'

In Megha and Kartik, I have found true friends—friends who are hard to find, difficult to leave and impossible to forget. Life wouldn't be the same without them.

I hope my mother can hear all these thoughts of mine. I even introduce Sahil to her as my boyfriend again. I hope she will love him as much as I do.

A part of me had got lost the day my mother had died. But today I have found that part again. I am whole again!

www.ingramcontent.com/pod-product-compliance
Lightning Source LLC
LaVergne TN
LVHW010316070526
838199LV00065B/5576